Nowaki

MICHIGAN MONOGRAPH SERIES IN JAPANESE STUDIES
NUMBER 72

CENTER FOR JAPANESE STUDIES
THE UNIVERSITY OF MICHIGAN

Nowaki

Natsume Sōseki

TRANSLATED AND WITH AN AFTERWORD AND CHRONOLOGY BY
WILLIAM N. RIDGEWAY

CENTER FOR JAPANESE STUDIES
THE UNIVERSITY OF MICHIGAN
ANN ARBOR   2011

Published by the Center for Japanese Studies,
The University of Michigan
1007 E. Huron St.
Ann Arbor, MI 48104-1690

Library of Congress Cataloging-in-Publication Data

Natsume, Soseki, 1867-1916.
   [Nowaki. English]
   Nowaki / Natsume Sōseki ; translated and with an afterword and
chronology by William N. Ridgeway.
       p. cm. — (Michigan monograph series in Japanese studies ; no. 72)
   ISBN 978-1-929280-68-1 (pbk. : alk. paper)
   I. Ridgeway, William N. II. Title. III. Series.

   PL812.A8N6813   2011
   895.6′342—dc22

                                                        2011013254

This book was set in Palatino Macron.

This publication meets the ANSI/NISO Standards for Permanence of Paper
for Publications and Documents in Libraries and Archives (Z39.48—1992).

Printed and bound by CPI Group (UK) Ltd, Croydon, CR0 4YY

To V.H.V.

Contents

Acknowledgments

I would like to thank the National Coalition of Independent Scholars for their support in the form of a Yosef Wosk Award, which was valuable to me in completing the research for this translation project. Additional thanks go to William Matsuda for his expert proofreading and helpful suggestions, and to Bruce Willoughby, CJS editor. Mention also must be made of a pony that was made available to me from Professor V. H. Viglielmo, who sometime in 1950 received an English translation of *Nowaki* from a Japanese scholar, whose name and whereabouts have disappeared from memory. I have benefitted greatly from his manuscript. And, finally, I wish to acknowledge the scholarship of Jim Reichert, whose writing on *Nowaki* first sparked my interest in this novel.

Nowaki

1

Shirai Dōya was a man of letters.

For eight years after graduating from the university he drifted from one teaching post to the next at two or three middle schools in the country, and in the spring of last year he aimlessly returned to Tokyo. The word "drift" applies to minstrels; "aimless" can also mean coming and going freely. The appropriateness of these phrases in describing Dōya's behavior, although a writer himself, is questionable. A tangled thread ends in a single strand but may have behind its individual terminus a multitude of twists and turns. Even geese flying north in autumn and swallows returning from the south in spring certainly have their reasons.

His first post was somewhere in Echigo, a place famous for its petroleum. Four or five blocks from school there was a large oil company. More than two-thirds of the town's prosperity was maintained by the company's largess. To the townspeople the company was worth more than several middle schools put together. Company directors were gentlemen due to their wealth; middle school teachers were perceived as inferior due to their poverty. If push came to shove between the wealthy gentlemen and the inferior teachers, the victor would be obvious to anyone. Dōya once gave a lecture on "The Power of Money and Moral Character," explaining why these two things were not necessarily compatible, and he implicitly admonished the company directors for their arrogance and the youth for their lack of conviction, stating the evils of vainly worshipping Mammon.

The company directors called him an impudent fellow. The town newspaper criticized him for being an incompetent teacher who had vented his conceited complaints. Even his colleagues thought him brash for his excessive behavior and for endangering the school's position. The school principal explained the relationship between the company and the school, and cautioned that it was unwise to make waves. Even his own students, in whom Dōya entrusted his last hopes, listened to their elders and began calling him a foolish teacher who did not know his place. Without a destination, Dōya left Echigo, drifting.

Then he migrated to Kyushu. Divided into two parts, Kyushu would be nothing without its industrial North. Here you do not qualify as human unless you are coated with coal smoke and breathe the blackened air. With their pale faces sticking out of coats shiny with soot, speaking this about the world and that about society, these future insignificant citizens of incalculably worthless unproductive remarks have little right to existence. They, the ones without rights, are permitted an existence through the compassionate munificence of the businessmen. For idle-talking scholars and teachers who are surrogate gramophones, where does the money come from to eke out a living month after month? A businessman claps his hands and out pours millions of yen, and those allowed to live by eating the crumbs are the scholars, the writers, and the teachers.

If you live by the power of money, slandering it is like abusing the parents by whom you were born and raised. "If you despise the businessmen who produce the money, then you should be prepared to starve to death. I am willing to experiment whether I will die or surrender before dying," said Dōya when dismissed from his duties. He then left Kyushu, drifting again.

His third post was in the countryside of Chūgoku. The atmosphere of this place was not so mercantile as before. But locals were so excessively territorial that they called people from other provinces "foreigners." Calling them "foreigners" was not so bad, but the locals sought to put them down by various underhanded means. If a dinner party were held, the locals would taunt them. If a lecture meeting were held, the locals would insinuate against them. The local newspaper would write sarcastically about them. Students would be prodded to tease their "foreign" teachers. And all this for no other reason than the apprehension that people from other provinces would not assimilate with them, the natives. Assimilation is undoubtedly an essential aspect of society. So much so that the French sociologist Jean Gabriel Tarde went so far as to say that society is mimesis. Assimilation may be important, and even Dōya himself realized the value of its importance. More than realized, he acknowledged the virtue of assimilation more than the man in the street, having obtained a high degree of education and possessing a broad view of society. The problem, however, was whether to assimilate with the higher or lower stratum of society. Assimilating without understanding this problem would bring no good to society. In his view, it would be a loss of honor.

One day the former village leader came to inspect the school. He was a lord and an aristocrat, and in the eyes of the local people, a god. When this god entered Dōya's classroom, Dōya continued with his lecture without giving him any particular notice. As for the god, he of course made no greeting. Then things got complicated. The classroom is sacred ground. Standing on his teaching platform, imparting knowledge, the teacher is like a samurai armored for the battlefield. No one, Dōya insisted—not even an aristocrat or a former lord—had the right to interrupt his class. On account of this claim, Dōya once again left his post, drifting. When he was leaving town the local people taunted him, calling him pigheaded. With insults hurled at his back, the man they called pigheaded left town, drifting again.

Having left his middle school position three times, Dōya wandered back to Tokyo and showed no sign of moving again. Tokyo is the most exigent of Japan's cities to live in. Even if he were receiving the same salary he earned in the country, he could not live comfortably there. How much more difficult it would be to pursue his teaching profession and live there with arms folded across his chest. Was there nothing he could do but turn himself into a mummy?

Dōya had a wife, and a woman called a wife has a right to be supported. Even if he himself was resigned to becoming a mummy, he could not let his wife starve to death. She was already dissatisfied prior to his apparent plan to starve himself to death.

When they were first about to leave Echigo, he talked with his wife about his situation in detail. "Well, there is certainly a case for what you say," she said, and began bravely packing up their belongings. When they were about to leave Kyushu, he had given her a full account of the situation. "The same story again?" she said, and fell silent. When they were about to leave Chūgoku, her words turned to admonishment: "If you remain obstinate like this, we will never settle down." In a seven-year period he had wandered three times, and his wife had grown farther away from him with each migration.

Had she grown farther away from him because of the moves or because of the loss of income? Suppose his salary had increased with each move. What then? Would she still have grumbled the words "If you remain obstinate . . ."? Suppose he had acquired a doctorate and been appointed professor at a university, would she still have repeated the words "If you remain obstinate . . ."? Without asking her opinion, none can say.

Had her attitude toward her husband suddenly changed because he had become a doctor of literature or a professor and had achieved an empty name acclaimed by an empty world, she, his wife, influenced by the rumbling of these things in her heart, could not be called a friend.

If a wife's estimation of her husband is subject to the world's estimation, she is no different from the person in the street. She is essentially the same person she was before getting married and before she knew his name. But in the eyes of her husband she was an utter stranger. If there is no change in a wife's knowledge of her husband before and after marriage, then she does not deserve to be called a wife. The world, however, is full of such unwifely wives. Did Dōya feel that his own wife belonged to this classification of wives? Were he to realize that his own wife, staying by his side at each move, did not understand him, how miserable that would be.

Indeed, the world, such as it is, is full of wives unworthy of the name. And while the world is full of wives unworthy of the name, couples seem to get along harmoniously. Those in favorable circumstances need not analyze the psychology of their wife to such an extent. In the case of contracting a skin disease, it is necessary to do dermatological research. But for a disease-free person to be shown something foul under a microscope and to be made to suffer without cause, would be to sling a muckrake for fun. When the situation is reversed, and the wheel of fortune turns from good to worse, any wedded couple will experience moments of disagreement. Even the bond between parent and child can snap under pressure. They realize that the beauty of their child is merely skin-deep. Who knows to what extent Dōya was conscious of this?

Dōya had not resigned his post three times expecting to fall deeper into trouble, much less to beset his innocent wife with grief. Nothing could be done: society did not accept him. If society did not accept him, why did he not try to make himself acceptable? He could not, because the moment he tried to be accepted he would be neatly annihilated. Dōya was confident that his moral character was higher than the average man's. The higher the character, the greater the responsibility to lift those lower than oneself to high moral ground. Knowing that one belongs to a higher plane and yet to descend to a lower one, is to take many years of education and bury the fruits of that education in the ground. Unless one wields the influence of his moral character over others, the moral character that one has taken pains to build would be as ineffectual as not having undertaken such a task to begin with, making the entire enterprise a futile one. Dōya had taught English, history, and once even ethics, and in doing so also communicated the art that he had accumulated through his character building. Had he made this art the sole purpose of his own education, he would have had to do nothing but stand in class before an open textbook. A teacher who is satisfied in teaching from the textbook and earning his living this way is no different in theory from a tightrope artist who earns his living crossing a tightrope or a baton twirler who earns his living twirling a baton. Education is different from tightrope crossing and baton twirling. The acquisition of knowledge is just the beginning of education; the true purpose is the building of human character. To size up the large and the small, to weigh the light and the heavy, to distinguish between good and evil, to always know right from wrong, wisdom from folly, truth from falsehood—that is the purpose of learning.

This was Dōya's conviction. Unashamed of selling his art, he nonetheless felt deeply debased for deviating from the fundamental principles of learning. Not being accepted where he worked was the result of his own attitude toward the true grounds of learning. He therefore did not feel dispirited as long as he saw no guilt when he looked inside his own heart. He could not have understood the abuse heaped upon him—"impertinent fool" they called him—had he held it in the palm of his hand and scrutinized it under a magnifying glass in the summer sun.

Three times he became a teacher and three times he was dismissed. Each time he thought he had made a great accomplishment, an accomplishment greater than his doctorate. A doctor of philosophy is perhaps something great, but it is still a title earned by devotion to the art of learning, not unlike the title of Junior Fifth Rank being conferred upon a rich man for his contribution to the naval shipbuilding fund. Dōya was dismissed because he was a man of high moral character. As a Western poet said, "The honest man is the noblest work of God." Every time he was dismissed from his post he said over and over in his heart the phrase, "He who keeps to the Way is even higher than a deity." His wife, however, had never heard the phrase from his lips. Nor would she have understood it had she heard it.

In as much as she was incapable of understanding, she grumbled at her husband long before the possibility of starving to death became a reality. Dōya was not indifferent to his wife's suffering. He was different from the ordinary husband only in his unwillingness to deviate from his own path in order to please his wife. The world calls him a man: by marrying, he becomes a husband; by associating with people, he becomes a friend; leading someone by the hand, he becomes an elder brother; being led by the hand, he becomes a younger brother. Living a public life, he may become a pioneer; entering a school building, he must become a teacher. All this is simply what is called a man. What a simple world it would be if being called a man were enough in the world. His wife lived in such a simple world. In her world, Dōya existed in no other capacity than as her husband—not a scholar, not a public-spirited individual, much less a man who went against the masses and lived by the Way. In her opinion, Dōya's worsening reputation at each turn was due to his incompetence; his resigning his position in each town was due to nothing more than his own capricious actions.

Dōya, who had come back to Tokyo after three consecutive caprices in the country, said to his wife that he would no longer seek work in the provinces, and declared that he would never become a teacher again. Disillusioned with the classroom, he realized that to reform his disillusionment with social conditions, he must resort to the power of the pen. Up until now, wherever he went and whatever occupation he pursued, he had thought that the crooked would give way, like flax bending at his touch, as long as he himself remained straight. Fame was not what he desired. Influence and popularity were not what he wished for. All he wanted was to show by his own exemplary behavior how to make the right choices, to mold the young generation into future citizens, to open their eyes to reform. Acting on his personal convictions for more than six years had resulted in utter failure. "There is a bit of kindness to be found everywhere," as the saying goes, and Dōya took for granted that people would gravitate toward the righteous, the noble, and the reasonable. "Next time, next time," he thought at each change of post during these past six plus years, the world would appreciate his endeavors, but his inexperience in the affairs of men yielded the miscalculation of a lifetime. The world was not so noble-minded as he imagined, and not so discriminating. On the contrary, appreciation followed after the rich and powerful like their own shadow. Overestimating a world not so advanced as he assumed, Dōya went to the provinces for the education of youth, but his work was like building a solid house on shaky ground, a house which, though quickly built, was quickly demolished by wind and rain. One cannot live peacefully in this world without preparing a foundation or, if possible, quell the elements. To make a world that one cannot inhabit peacefully a habitable place is the enterprise of a public-minded individual.

For a public-minded individual, who lacks money or power, to accomplish his lofty enterprise, he must rely on the power of the ink brush, trust in the power of speech, and rack his brain for the wisdom of altruism. But the brain will be exhausted, the tongue tired from talking, brushes broken, and for all that the world remains indifferent to his appeals.

Be that as it may, even a public-minded individual cannot exert himself without a livelihood. Even if he were prepared to starve, his wife would never consent to starvation. A husband who does not provide for his wife is a great sinner in her eyes. When Dōya and his wife left the provinces this spring and arrived in Tokyo, they stayed at a cheap inn in Shibakotohiracho, at which the following conversation took place between them.

"You say you are giving up the teaching profession. What do you plan on taking up next?"

"I have no clear plan yet. But something will turn up in due time."

"'Something will turn up.' Isn't that a bit vague?"

"Yes, it is quite indefinite, I suppose."

"I am troubled to find you so unconcerned. You are a man, so you can afford to speak in such a way. But I do wish you would be more sympathetic toward me and understand my perspective."

"That's why I said I have decided not to go to the provinces any more and not to become a teacher again."

"You are free to make up your own mind, but what shall we do if you cannot decide on a fixed income?"

"You will be satisfied, I hope, if I earn a sufficient sum of money, though it may not be a monthly salary."

"If you earn a sufficient sum of money, that would be quite satisfactory."

"The question is settled then."

"Then you are sure you can earn the money?"

"Well, I should hope so."

"But how?"

"I am considering that just now. We have just arrived—how could I make a plan so soon?"

"Which is why I am so anxious. You say you have decided to stay in Tokyo, but that alone does not constitute a plan."

"My, you are a worrywart."

"Of course I'm worried. Wherever we went you would quarrel with people. If I'm a worrywart, you are quarrelsome."

"Perhaps I am. But my quarrels are…Well, enough of that. I will do something or other so we can live in Tokyo."

"Why don't you go to your elder brother and ask for his assistance?"

"Well, that may be the thing to do, but he is not the kind of man to take interest in other people's affairs."

"Oh, how like you to decide on everything! Just yesterday did he not say many kind things when he came to visit?"

"Yesterday? Yes, yesterday he said he would exert himself on our behalf. He did say that."

"What was wrong with that?"

"*Nothing is wrong with that*. He is welcome to his fine talk. But he may prove to be undependable."

"Why?"

"Why? Wait and see."

"In that case, you had better ask your friends for some help. Why not start tomorrow?"

"Friends you say? I have no friends to speak of in this city. All my colleagues from school days are scattered here and there."

"What about Adachi-san, who sends you New Year's greetings regularly. He is doing very well in Tokyo, is he not?"

"Adachi? The professor?"

"Yes. But you are too proud, so you make yourself disliked by everybody. Is there something wrong with being a professor? It is an excellent position."

"Is that so? Then I shall go to Adachi and seek his assistance. But if I can come up with some money by other means, there is no need to visit him, is there?"

"There you go again. Talking that way. You *are* stubborn."

"Yes, I am a stubborn one."

2

The afternoon sun of autumn bore down on him, seeming to penetrate his hat to his skull and producing a cheerful mood. All the park benches, because they were free of charge, were monopolized. Takayanagi had already circled Hibiya Park three times in search of an unoccupied one. Finding not a single bench waiting for him in spite of his search, he directed his heavy feet toward the main entrance. At that moment a young man of Takayanagi's age happened to be coming from the opposite direction.

"Hello!"

"Hello!" said Takayanagi, making the same greeting.

"Where have you been?" asked the young man.

"I have been round and round the entire park to find a place to rest, but all the seats are taken. Where places to sit are free to the public, the public has already sat. They do not miss a trick."

"It is because the weather is so fine. Yes, I see there are a lot of people out today. Over there! Look at the one walking around the bamboo grove toward the fountain."

"Who? That woman? Someone you know?"

"How would I know someone like that?"

"Then why should I look at her?"

"The color of her kimono!"

"She is rather splendidly dressed."

"That color shows to its best advantage against the background of the bamboo. Moreover, it does not really stand out until seen through the transparent air of autumn."

"Is that so?"

"Do you not find it so yourself?"

"Not particularly. But I admit it is pretty."

"What a pity to call it merely pretty. You do intend to become a writer, don't you?

"Yes, of course."

"In that case, you will have to be more sensitive."

"Why? There is no need to be sensitive in that regard when there is so much more to be sensitive about."

"Ha, ha, ha! It is all very well to be self-confident. Now that we've had the pleasure of meeting her, will you mind walking around once more?"

"I've had quite enough walking for today. In fact, unless I go home directly by train I shall be in danger of missing my lunch."

"What do you say to my treating you to lunch?"

"Well, perhaps some other time."

"But why? You don't like the idea of having lunch with me?"

"It's not that. It's not that at all. I hesitate because I am treated by you so frequently."

"Ha, ha! No need to stand on ceremony. Come along!" The young man dragged Takayanagi to a Western-style restaurant in the park, where they took their seats in the upstairs dining room with a commanding view.

Waiting for their orders to come, Takayanagi looked down wearily on the passersby, resting his elbows on the table and cupping his pale face in his hands. The other young man mumbled to himself, "This is quite spacious!" "They seem to be doing a brisk business." "What a strange place for a mirror with advertising on it." Then, putting his hand in his trouser pocket, he cried, "Dear me! I forgot to buy cigarettes!"

"I have some," said Takayanagi, digging out a pack of Shikishima brand and offering them across the white tablecloth.

Just at that moment a waitress brought their order, before he had time to light up.

"This is draft beer. Let's offer a toast with it!" said the young man, downing a gulp of the white foam rising from the amber bottom.

"But to what do we toast?" asked Takayanagi, taking a drink.

"To our graduation!"

"It's been some time since our graduation," said Takayanagi, placing his glass on the table.

"Graduation comes but once in one's life; it can be celebrated any number of times!"

"As it takes place only once in one's life, it is hardly worth celebrating."

"Just the opposite of me. Miss! What is this fried fish? Salmon, is it? Squeeze your orange over this part," he said, squeezing the wedge between his thumb and index finger and dribbling the juice over the fish. The liquid was quickly absorbed into the fish like a light shower dissolves into dry ground.

"Is the orange wedge for that purpose? I thought it was a garnish."

Sitting below the mirror advertising Sapporo Beer, two pretentious-looking men burst into laughter. Takayanagi, still holding his orange wedge, gave them a disgusted look, but the men did not mind his stare.

"Yes, I'll go. I'll go any time. Hee, hee, hee. Let's go tonight! Am I too eager? Ha, ha, ha, ha, ha."

"Hee, hee, hee, I was joking. Actually, I meant to ask you to come with me tonight. Eh? Ha, ha, ha. Not up to it? Ha, ha, ha. You know what kind of woman she is. I can't keep up with her! Hee, hee, hee. Aha, ha, ha, ha."

The reflection in the advertising mirror of two ruddy faces, like the bottom of terracotta pots, contorted and compressed, expanded and contracted, in utter disregard of the shocked diners. Turning his loathing gaze away from them, Takayanagi looked at his friend.

"They are merchants," said the latter in a low voice.

"They are businessmen, I see," whispered Takayanagi, and gave up squeezing the orange wedge.

The terracotta pots paid the bill, teased the waitress, and left, talking in loud voices as if they owned the place.

"You know, Nakano . . . "

"Hmmm?" he mumbled, stuffing his mouth with chicken.

"What do the likes of them think of the world, I wonder?"

"They think nothing of the world. They merely live their lives, carrying on that way."

"I envy them. How could I—? Well, it's impossible."

"It's no good envying people like that. Now I understand why you did not join me in a toast to our graduation. Cheer up, and let us have another drink!"

"I don't envy people like that. I envy them their leisure. It is true I have graduated, but if one has to work hard for one's daily bread as I do, one owes few thanks to one's graduation."

"Is that the case with you? As for me, I cannot help rejoicing. We have our whole lives ahead of us! There is no point in being depressed from the very start."

"Yes, our real life is just beginning, but I cannot help feeling depressed when faced with the uncertainty of the future."

"But why? You have no reason to be pessimistic. Do the best you can. So will I. Together we can try. And in preparation for that, let us eat nourishing food—Western cookery! Here's our beefsteak now. This is the last course. They say a rare beefsteak is easy to digest, you know. How about this one?" asked Nakano wielding a knife and slicing his thick piece of beef down the middle. "Oh yes, it's red. See how red inside. The blood is oozing out!"

Takayanagi said nothing, but fell to devouring his portion. In spite of the redness of the beefsteak, he doubted its digestibility.

When one attempts to air one's complaints to a friend, one feels disappointed if the other party offers half-hearted consolation before one has made a clean breast of it. One is not sure whether one is understood or not, whether the sympathy offered is sincere or mere lip service. Looking at the redness of his steak, Takayanagi wondered how Nakano's sensitiveness could be so rough-edged. It was Nakano's usual practice to throw a wet blanket over Takayanagi just when he was trying to make a point. Were Nakano an unkind, cold-hearted man by nature, Takayanagi would have been prepared from the beginning and would not have been taken by surprise at such a cold reception. Were Nakano such a man, Takayanagi would not regret being frustrated by him. But in Takayanagi's eyes, Nakano Kiichi was a promising young man, beautiful and wise, kind-hearted and sensible. Takayanagi could not understand how this promising young man could do such an inconsiderate thing from time to time.

They had attended the same high school and lived together in the same dormitory, with their desks side by side facing the same window; they entered the same Department of Literature, attended lectures of the same professor, and graduated together the same year, this very summer. There were dozens of graduates from the same department this year, but there were no two friends as intimate as Takayanagi and Nakano.

Takayanagi was regarded as a sarcastic pessimist, taciturn and unsociable. Nakano was a bright youth, generous, sociable, and having refined tastes. Once they became acquainted, their intercourse quickly ripened into a friendship so close as to cause suspicion in others. Their fate was intertwined like the inside and outside of a seamlessly woven garment with an Oshima facing and a Chichibu lining.

When there is only a single intimate person in the world, and no other to replace him, he is your father, your brother, and your lover. For Takayanagi, Nakano was not a mere friend. Takayanagi was disappointed in Nakano's not listening to his complaint to the end, and all the more displeased by his unfelt consolation, for his having rubbed salt in his wound.

But Takayanagi's dissatisfaction with Nakano was unwarranted. One cannot blame a Hina doll for not competing with a geisha and then fail to comprehend the Hina doll's love. Nakano was born into a well-to-do family and raised in a happy home; he knew no more of the world's trouble than a man knows about a rainstorm observed through windowpanes as he sits comfortably at his quilt-covered brazier. He could appreciate the pattern of fine Yuzen, the luster of gold-leaf screens, burning candles in silver stands. How much more sensitive was his eye to the beauty of women. Nor was he an uncivilized savage who knew nothing of filiality toward one's parents, affection for one's siblings, and trust in one's friends. The sun had always shone brightly upon the hemisphere he inhabited. One who lives on the bright side has no knowledge of the dark hemisphere under one's feet other than that learned in geography. Even while walking, he may not be aware of the opposite side of the earth upon which his feet rest, never to shudder at the thought of the utter darkness. Takayanagi was a lonely inhabitant of the dark side. There was no more to their association than having in common the circumstances of treading the same earth from opposite hemispheres. The finely woven fabric of their relationship, the Oshima facing and the Chichibu lining, was held together by a slender thread. By undoing the slender

13

thread, the two sections fall apart into cloth woven in Kagoshima and cloth woven in Saitama, two points separated by hundreds of miles. When one has a bad tooth one goes directly to a dentist, not to a friend who has no experience with a toothache. For he may tell you that you have a right to feel such pain, and offer no consolation whatsoever.

"That is all fine for you. You have no need to be pessimistic," said Takayanagi, who, giving up the remaining half of his beefsteak, puffing smoke from his Shikishima cigarette, looked at Nakano as he spoke. Nakano, chewing his food, shook his head together with his right hand, signaling his disagreement.

"You say I need not be pessimistic. Having no need for pessimism then means one is a fool."

Takayanagi moved his thin lips, smiling faintly, but the ripple soon disappeared without spreading to his cheeks. Nakano continued talking.

"Just three years ago during my university days I read a few books of philosophy and literature. Whatever you may think of me, I think I know how pessimistic human life is."

"What you know from books, that is," said Takayanagi as if standing on a high mountain looking down at someone in the valley.

"Yes, from books, but also from having pain, from grief."

"But you live a comfortable life. You have abundant leisure. You can study as much as you like and publish as you wish. You are happiness itself compared to me," said Takayanagi, this time with a slight air of envy.

"I am not all that happy. I have so many worries that I grow weary of life," said Nakano emphatically, asserting his claim to anxiety.

"Do you?" replied Takayanagi skeptically.

"If you too do not take me seriously, I am indeed wretched. As a matter of fact, I intended on calling on you today to find consolation in your sympathy."

"I cannot sympathize with you without knowing of your situation."

"I shall tell you, by and by. I felt so depressed I had to go out for a walk. You ought to be a bit more understanding."

At this Takayanagi smiled openly. Even his intention to show a bit more understanding required more explanation than this.

"And why have _you_ been walking about the park today?" asked Nakano, looking at Takayanagi's face.

"There is something strange about your face. The right side in the sunlight looks very ruddy, whereas the left side in the shadows looks unhealthy. Strange. As if your face on either side of your nose is trying to contradict itself. Your face appears as a conjoining of half a mask of tragedy and half a mask of comedy," declared Nakano without taking a breath.

Listening to this innocent remark, Takayanagi felt as if his secrets had been read through his features. He gasped and rubbed his right hand several times in a circular motion from forehead to chin, as if to erase the contradiction in his face.

"As pleasant as the weather is, I've no time to spare for a walk. Today I had to go to the Lost Property Office past Shinbashi to recover a lost article, and on my way home I entered the park to take a rest," answered Takayanagi, resting his head in the hand he had just rubbed his face with, and looking depressed as before. Since he had rubbed out the conjoined masks of the tragedy and comedy sides of his face, the result ought to have been his normal face, but a strange grimy element remained.

"Lost article? What have you lost?"

"Yesterday I left my manuscript behind on the train."

"Your manuscript? That is a calamity. I cannot feel at ease with a manuscript until it appears in print. For us a manuscript is more precious than life."

"I wish I had the time to write such precious manuscripts. It's hopeless," said Takayanagi in a self-deprecatory tone.

"What kind of manuscript was it?"

"It was my translation of *How to Teach Geography*. I promised to deliver the copy by tomorrow. Now if I've lost it, I won't get paid. I shall have to do the job over again. I am miserable, indeed."

"And having went looking for it, you failed to recover the thing?"

"Yes, I have failed."

"But what may have become of it?"

"Perhaps the conductor took it home and made a duster out of the paper."

"I think not. But what a loss if it doesn't turn up."

"I am resigned to the loss because it came from my own carelessness. But the man in charge at the Lost Property Office was a loathsome fellow— very unkind and bureaucratic. After reeling off the usual office retort, he answered uniformly each of my questions with the rejoinder, 'I don't know.' He is your typical Japanese of the twentieth century. The president of the tram company must be the same sort of man, I am sure."

"How exasperating for you. But all people are not like the clerk at the Lost Property Office."

"Give me more humane examples then."

"Cynical, aren't you."

"The world is full of cynicism. The world today is an open competition of cold-heartedness," Takayanagi said, throwing the butt of his Shikishima over the second floor railing at the same moment when thank yous were heard from below. Leaving the restaurant were two men wearing trilbies, and into one fell by chance the burning cigarette butt. The man with the burning hat strutted away.

"Look what an outrageous thing you've done," Nakano said.

"It was a mistake. I see they are the two businessmen from before. Who cares? Let it be."

"Yes, the same two. Why were they so long in leaving? They may have been playing billiards."

"They may be up to something. They are the same sort of people as the Lost Property clerk."

"He has noticed his hat's on fire. He has taken it off and is beating out the fire!"

"Ha, ha, ha! What a farce!" said Takayanagi with a merry laugh.

"You are quite malicious, aren't you," said Nakano.

"Well, I admit I was wrong. Even if it was an accident, finding satisfaction in a vengeful moment was lowly of me. To be pleased about it belittles the value of a Bachelor of Arts," Takayanagi said, relapsing into a gloomy mood.

"Quite so," Nakano said, in a tone of half reproach and half approval.

"But I am a Bachelor of Arts in name only. The truth of the matter is I am a hack writer. I am chagrined to think that though I am a university graduate, I have to work as a ghostwriter translating *How to Teach Geography*. Besides, I have parents who waited for my graduation with great hopes for me, and I am sorry to have disappointed them. But judging from my present circumstances, it is not likely that the day will soon come when their hopes will be met, though they may wait still longer."

"But we have only recently graduated. How is it possible to build a reputation so quickly? In the course of time we shall produce splendid works and once we've come into our own, the world will be our oyster!"

"And when might that be?"

"Don't be so impatient! By and by, regeneration will take place. We must persevere until our time comes around. You can be sure that the public gradually will recognize our true merit. Even I, such as I am, have caught the public eye by continually contributing to magazines."

"That's all well and good for you. You can afford to write whenever you like. In my case, I have any number of things I want to write about, but I have absolutely no time for putting them on paper. This is my greatest regret. Had I a patron so that I might work under comfortable circumstances, I would show you a great work. Or at least if I could bring home sixty yen a month I should be satisfied. True, I had been self-supporting during my student days, but I never dreamed that I should have to struggle to keep myself alive after graduation."

"Your hardships are regrettable. If I could freely dispose of our family fortune, I would gladly become your patron."

"I wish you would. I am utterly at a loss. Even the position of a middle school teacher in the country is not all that easy to secure."

"That may be so."

"A friend of mine, for example, graduated from the philosophy course three years ago and is still unemployed."

"Is that so?"

"Looking back, I remember committing a wrong as an ignorant child. But, on the other hand, times were better in those days, so perhaps middle school teaching positions were not as difficult to secure."

"But what on earth did you do?"

"At the middle school in my native town there was a teacher of English called Shirai Dōya."

"Dōya, that's an unusual name. Sounds more like the name of an iron kettle."

"I'm not sure how to pronounce the name correctly. But we always called him Dōya. This Dōya-sensei—he was also a Bachelor of Arts—was driven away from the school by us."

"How?"

"We simply drove him away by harassing him. He was a good teacher. But we were too young to judge his character. I don't think he was a bad man."

"Then why did you drive him away?"

"Well, you must know that there were some wicked middle school teachers back then. And they egged us on. I can still recall that we would go in a group of fifteen or sixteen at night, let out a battle cry and charge Dōya-sensei's house and throw stones."

"How barbarous! Why did you do such a silly thing?"

"I don't know why. We did it only for fun. Probably none of us could tell you why we did it."

"Very thoughtless, I should say."

"Yes, it was thoughtless of me. The only people who knew the reason were the teachers who incited us. And they only told us to do it because he was presumptuous."

"How cruel! Are there such wicked ones among teachers?"

"There certainly were. Perhaps because they could use children to do their bidding. But they existed."

"And what became of Dōya-sensei?"

"He resigned from his post."

"What a pity."

"I truly regret having done such a thing. I am sure he suffered many hardships in seeking a new post. If I ever happen to meet him, I will sincerely apologize to him."

"Where is he now?"

"I don't know."

"Then you are not sure when you will see him next."

"But I may meet him quite unexpectedly any day. Or, it is also possible that he may have died from starvation, unable to find another teaching job. I remember his coming to the classroom before he resigned to say something."

"Well, what did he say?"

"'Boys! We teachers should not live in order to teach, but should live for the cause of the Way! The Way is higher than anything else in the world. One who has yet to realize this truth is not a man in the real sense of the term. Do your best to understand the truth!'"

"Really!"

"At his words all of us burst out laughing, saying 'Ain't he cocky! Ain't he cocky!' But I wonder who was the cocky party."

"What rather absurd goings-on one has in country schools!"

"Absurd things take place in Tokyo, too. And it's not only at schools—the whole world is that way. It makes me weary."

"Well, we've gone on for some time now. What do you say to coming with me to the Myoka-en in Shinagawa?"

"But for what?"

"To see the flowers."

"But I must go home and work on my translation of *How to Teach Geography*."

"You must amuse yourself once in a while. If you go to such a beautiful place you will enter a pleasant frame of mind and be able to work better on your translation."

"Perhaps you're right. Are you going there simply for amusement?"

"Not entirely for amusement. I want to do a sketch there to use for material."

"Material for what?"

"I'll show you when it's finished. I'm writing a novel. In one of its chapters I intend to describe a scene where a girl in a garden is looking intently at a red flower, which under her gaze grows paler and paler in color until it becomes completely white."

"A fantasy?"

"Well, I want to write something that is both fantastic and mysterious, which can somehow induce in the reader a mood of yearning for a remote past. I wonder if I can achieve the sort of effect I am striving for. Please be kind enough to read it and give me your opinion when it is done."

"Myoka-en is not the sort of place to resort to for such inspiration. You would do better to go home and look at some pictures by Holman Hunt.

Oh, how I too long to write something I have in mind. But I haven't the time for it."

"It is too bad that you have such disdain for natural beauty."

"Who gives a fig about Nature? In this severe world of the twentieth-century we cannot afford to pay such regard to Nature. What I wish to write is not such dreamy stuff as yours. Mine may not be pretty, but on the contrary it may be painful, stinging to read, yet I shall be satisfied if it should reveal my innermost feelings. Whether it is poetical or not, I do not care. I will have written well if I stab myself hard enough for the pain to make me jump and I am able to convey that pain to the reader, to make him say, 'That hurt!' I wish to enlighten the comfortable and complacent to the reality that can find no expression in their deepest dreams. I want to open the eyes of the debauchee to the essence of man, so that he may confess with bowed head that he had never entertained such a thought before but now acknowledges it to be undeniably true. —A different direction entirely from yours."

"Yet such literature would make the reader uncomfortable. —Of course you are at liberty to write as you please. Why not come along to Myoka-en with me?"

"If I could spare the time to go to the garden, I would rather write even a page of what I wish to declare. When I think of it I cannot help but feel restless. Really I cannot afford to idle away my precious time eating rare beef steaks!"

"Ha, ha, ha, ha! You are getting impatient again. You need not be. See! There are people in this world like those businessmen we just saw."

"Those kind make me all the more eager to get to work. Had I but one-tenth of their time and money, I could produce something to show the world."

"Then you will not consent to accompany me to the gardens?"

"No, because then I shall have to go home in the evening. You have on your winter suit whereas I still wear my summer one, so I am liable to catch cold."

"Ha, ha, ha, ha! You have invented a far-fetched excuse. It is time one put on winter clothes. Why have you not changed your clothes for winter? You are lazy in everything."

"It is not due to my laziness. I have no winter suit to change into. For that matter I have not yet paid a penny on this one."

"Oh, I see," Nakano said, looking sorry.

By this time all the other lunchtime guests were gone, and as Takayanagi and Nakano rose from their chairs, they left behind breadcrumb-littered table-cloths, here and there looking desolate. Outside the restaurant it was livelier than before. Men and women still occupied all the benches. The heat of the autumn sun penetrated the back of the coats of the two friends.

3

Entering through a gate with a cypress door and a silver-tiled roof, he walked about ten paces along granite steppingstones that had been sprinkled with water. The stone steps came to an end at the front entrance of a mansion. A frosted-glass door looked solemnly shut as if closed against the encroaching autumn. No sound disturbed the silence of the big house.

He pushed the ivory button on the polished, spindle-wood doorpost, and heard footsteps approaching and the sound of doors unlocking. The doors were pulled back left and right, revealing a concrete floor with a mirror-like surface. On the right was an imitation Chinese red earthenware pot about a foot in diameter and containing two or three hemp palms standing quietly. On the raised floor was a gold-leaf screen about four-feet high on which was depicted Kokaji of Sanjo, forging a blade with a supernatural being in disguise as his partner, praying that he might produce a sword for the emperor.

A polite maidservant of eighteen or nineteen came out to greet the visitor. Receiving a card bearing the name Shirai Dōya, she asked, "You wish to see the young master?" Dōya cocked his head to one side and thought for a moment, for he had never met either Nakano the elder or Nakano the younger, and it was quite possible he could be refused an interview. He was entirely ignorant about this Mr. Nakano, so without meeting him he could not tell if the person he had come to interview was young or old, and, if he failed to see him, he would remain ignorant about him for the rest of his life. Dōya had been turned away several times in the past, before he had a chance to find out what sort of man he had come to see, whether he was lame or one-eyed. If he were not to be turned away again, he must answer the maid's question. Being forced to decide on an indifferent question one way or another is a sort of tax that is levied on the wise by the foolish.

"I should like to see the one who has graduated from the university," said Dōya, but realizing that it was possible that the father was also a university graduate, he corrected himself, "I mean the one who is a writer."

The maid said nothing, but made a bow, stood up and went in. Dōya noticed that the soles of her white socks were soiled. Above him hung a spherical cast-iron lamp, which had an openwork design of sandpipers flying over waves, papered on the inside. While looking at the long chain which attached the lamp to the ceiling. Dōya wondered how they would light the lamp.

The maid returned and said, "This way please." Leaving behind on the elegant step stone his geta, indented by his big toe and having a loose thong,

Dōya followed the maid, whose lank body resembled a snake gourd.

The reception room was decorated in Western style. A round table was draped rather carelessly with a cloth, into which was woven a design of five or six roses in subdued colors. The borders of the cloth fell in folds onto a carpet of similar colors in such a way that one could not tell where one ended and the other began. The fireplace was still in disuse, concealed behind a small two-leaf folding screen placed one foot in front of it. Maroon damask curtains clashed with the general color scheme of the decoration, but this fact escaped Dōya's notice. Sensei had never in his life been in such as fine room as this.

Sensei looked up at a framed picture on the wall. Depicted was a Kyoto dancing girl clad in a long-sleeved Yuzen kimono and playing a hand-drum. Even the tip of her little finger was precisely rendered, her right hand poised just at the moment her white fingers sprang back from tapping the drum. But Dōya-sensei was not one to appreciate such things. He thought only that it was in bad taste to hang such a painting on the wall. In the opposite corner stood an art nouveau styled bookcase in which some luxuriously bound Western books with gold letters on their spines were exposed to sunbeams filtering through the curtains. It was splendid, but Dōya did not give it the slightest attention.

Nakano appeared wearing a cotton-filled pongee kimono bound with a crepe obi. Looking slyly at Dōya over his gold-rimmed spectacles, he said, "I am sorry to have kept you waiting," and sat down.

Dōya had on a cheap common silk kimono, a black cotton coat with family crests, and a divided skirt of inferior silk. With his hands still in his pockets he said, "I am sorry to trespass on your precious time." His attitude was cool and self-possessed.

After the initial greetings, Nakano continued to feel shy but built up the courage to say, "So you are Shirai Dōya?" he asked with great curiosity. Nakano could assume as much by just looking at the calling card, but being an inexperienced writer fresh from the university, he put this unnecessary question to Dōya.

"Yes," said Dōya-sensei calmly. Nakano felt discouraged, for as soon as he saw the name on the card he was reminded with surprise that Dōya was the middle school teacher who had been expelled by his pupils. So when he found before him the very man miserably attired, he would have liked to ascertain, "Are you the Shirai-san who was harassed by middle school boys?" Yet all his sympathy would be wasted if he had the wrong Shirai. In order to establish the identity of the object of his sympathy, he had to ask, "Are you Dr. Shirai Dōya?" His well-intended interrogative proved futile when it met with a cool, indifferent reply: "Yes." The inexperienced writer had neither wit nor courage to say anything more.

"Please pardon me for taking the liberty of calling on you, but I have a favor to ask of you," said Dōya, picking up the conversation. A person with a request is a proper object of sympathy. For a person having no request to make of another, there is no competition for sympathy.

"I will do anything in my power for you," Nakano said, willingly.

"Our magazine, *The World*, plans to publish a symposium of opinions of eminent persons on how to resolve the anguish of today's young generation. But seeing how interviewing only influential persons would be uninteresting, the editorial staff decided to seek the opinions of some rising writers and critics as well. For this purpose I have been charged to interview you. If you don't mind, I should like to take notes."

Dōya-sensei then quietly took out a notebook and pencil from his breast pocket. He did not look eager to take notes, however, nor was he inclined to urge Nakano to speak. Neither did he think it worthwhile to solicit the opinion of such a young man about such a silly matter.

"I see," said the young man, raising his bright eyes to meet Dōya's, but seeing the expression on his face, as insipid as stale beer, he looked down again, drawing out the word, "Well . . ."

"What is your opinion on the subject, if I may ask," said Dōya out of a sense of duty, and ready to leave if there was none.

"Well, even if I have an opinion of my own, I hardly think it is worth being printed in your magazine."

"On the contrary. It will do very well."

"I wonder from whom you have heard about me. One cannot give a systematic opinion at a moment's notice, after all."

"I was told that our magazine's proprietor had come across your name in various periodicals from time to time."

"It's nothing, really," said Nakano, turning aside.

"Please say whatever you wish."

"Very well," said Nakano, hesitating and looking outside the window. "Where to begin?"

"I am ready," said Dōya, taking up his pencil.

"The word 'anguish' is in vogue now. It is, for the most part, a temporary thing, experienced by the weak-willed. Anguish of this sort has existed since the beginning of human history and will continue to exist to the very end. So, it is not worth discussing in my opinion."

"Hmm!" said Dōya, looking down and busily plying his pencil. The rustling sound of writing on paper was distinctly heard.

"On the other hand, there is a deeper form of anguish that young people never fail to experience, destined by nature as they are to undergo it."

Then there was an interval when the sound of the pencil alone was audible.

"That is—love."

Dōya stopped writing and looked at the speaker with an odd expression. Nakano felt unnerved, as if recalling the eccentric nature of his remark, but taking heart, he resumed. "What I call 'love' may seem strange to you. And nowadays people hesitate to speak of romantic love. This type of anguish is a positive fact, and one cannot but submit to a fact."

Dōya-sensei again looked up. But the long pale face he saw was completely calm and composed, and therefore it was impossible to read what was in his heart.

"Of all the anguish one experiences in a lifetime, there is none so serious, so severe, and so violent as that of love. Because it is such a powerful force, once we enter into the flames of anguish, we undergo a complete metamorphosis."

"Did you say metamorphosis?"

"Yes, a change of form—a transformation. One may have been leading a life adrift, unaware of one's relations to the world, living an idle existence, but then suddenly one becomes lucid."

"Lucid?"

"One becomes fully conscious of his own life. He feels most powerfully that he is alive. Love is no different from anguish. Experiencing love without anguish, one cannot speak of being fully conscious of life. Unless one goes through this purgatory, he cannot hope to enter paradise. Mere optimism will not do. Optimism attained without first tasting the bitterness of love and thereby affirming the significance of existence is a false optimism. The anguish of love, likewise, cannot be resolved any other way—only through love. Love causes anguish, but it also leads us to salvation."

"That should be adequate," Dōya said, looking up a third time.

"But I still have more to say. . . ."

"I would like to hear more, but the magazine intends to carry the opinions of a number of people, and I should regret having yours elided."

"Well then, I will stop here. This is my first experience of this kind, so I'm afraid you've had a difficult time taking notes."

"Not at all," said Dōya-sensei, putting away his notebook.

The youth thought that his declamation must have impressed the interviewer, and expected to hear a word of praise. But the listener merely replied, "Not at all," in his customary nonchalant attitude.

"I am sorry to have encroached on your precious time," the guest said, rising to go.

"Can you stay a little longer?" said Nakano in an attempt to detain him. At least a comment or criticism was in order. Not only that, he was curious about Takayanagi's story he had heard in Hibiya Park the other day. And Nakano had all the time in the world. He was a man of leisure.

"No, I'm in a bit of a hurry," said the guest, taking a step away from the table. As desirous of company as Nakano was, he resigned himself to the situation and bowed. Seeing his guest to the door, Nakano ventured to satisfy his curiosity by asking, "Do you happen to know a Takayanagi Shūsaku?"

"Takayanagi? I don't think so," answered Dōya, turning his long body half around, as one foot stepped down on the concrete floor from the stepstone.

"He graduated from the university this year."

"Then I cannot possibly know him," replied Dōya, placing the other foot on the concrete floor.

As Nakano was about to say something, they heard the clattering of a rickshaw along the pavement and the lowering of its shaft outside the glass door. The moment Dōya-sensei opened the door, a foot in leather-soled sandals descended lightly from the vehicle onto the granite paving stones. Feeling as though a multicolored cloud had passed before his eyes, he came out into the street.

It was four o'clock in the afternoon. In the dark jade-colored sky tinged with a light sepia there was an obscure shape of a kite circling around. Wild geese had not yet been seen this autumn. Some boys with their divided skirts tucked up came by singing merrily. They carried a bamboo branch slung over their shoulders, from which an owl made from pampas grass was hanging and dancing. Perhaps they had been on an excursion to Zoshigaya. Inside a fruit dealer's shop with low-hanging eaves, only the gleam of persimmons was visible. Toward evening the air felt chilly.

When Dōya came in front of the Yakuōji temple, he could barely distinguish from under the rim of his hat the faces of passersby in the street. Passing a stone marker inscribed on the right-hand side with the words "One of the Thirty-Three Temples for Pilgrimage," he then headed west at the corner with a dyer's shop on a side street. Walking about half a block, he arrived at the door of his house. It was dark inside.

"Oh, welcome home, dear," said his wife from the kitchen. The house was so small that the kitchen and the vestibule were not separated by much space.

"Has the maid gone somewhere?" asked Dōya, entering the six-mat drawing room from the two-mat vestibule.

"She went on an errand to Yanagichō," his wife replied and returned to the kitchen.

Taking in hand an oil lamp from a corner inside the alcove, he went onto the veranda and set to cleaning the lamp. With some manuscript paper he wiped the oil-container and the glass chimney and trimmed the blackened wick. Then, crumpling the paper into a ball, he threw it into the garden. Darkness had fallen, so that nothing in the garden could be seen.

Sitting down at his desk, he struck a match and lighted the lamp instantly. The whole room became light. For Sensei's sake, it would have been better if the room remained in darkness, for there was an alcove in name only that served no ornamental purpose. Contrary to convention, instead of a hanging scroll were piles of books, manuscripts, and notebooks. On his simple desk, looking more like a large offering stand used in Shinto shrines, lay nothing but an inkbottle and a cheap ink-stone. Either Dōya-sensei had no need for decorative objects, or, even if necessary, he could not afford them. It was plain to see, however, that in his humble, unheated room, Dōya-sensei had the equanimity to placidly grind his ink-stone against all odds. Perhaps he was living for something that had nothing to do with ornamentation. The plainer this indisputable fact became, the more unpleasant it was for his wife. Woman lives and dies for the sake of ornament. Most women go so far as to regard love itself as a form of decoration, in spite of the fact that love sustains their destiny. If love is their decoration, then it goes without saying that so also are their lovers. Not only that, but they regard themselves as ornaments, and thus if some people do not regard them as such, they consider those people stupid in their opinion. Though this is the honest view of life held by most women, they are not conscious of it. So when they discover their surroundings in entangled circumstances or encounter people who do not serve their ornamental purposes, they feel displeasure. When they vent their displeasure and yet have no power to change their circumstances or the people around them, the displeasure reflected in their eyes is dispersed in all directions, inciting them to change. They become more and more persistent in their incitement, radiating their displeasure in elaborate forms. Now the question had become how far had Dōya's wife progressed in this process. But being a woman of the ordinary type, it was natural that she should proceed in this direction as a consequence of breathing in the unornamented atmosphere. Or perhaps she had already advanced in that direction.

Before long Dōya-sensei removed his notebook from his breast pocket and began copying its contents onto manuscript paper. He was still wearing his split skirt trousers. He was still being ceremonious. He copied out the proposition of Nakano Kiichi on romantic love. Love and this very room, love and Dōya-sensei, were strictly incompatible. What thoughts were running through his mind as he copied from his notebook? People are various. The world too is various. It is only natural that this various world and its various people move in various ways. But it is simply that those who move broadly prevail over those who move deeply. Copying out his note in this formal manner, did Dōya regard himself as smaller and shallower than that theorist of romantic love behind the gold-rimmed spectacles? From behind the alcove a cricket chirruped.

His wife slid open the fusuma but Dōya paid her no attention. "My, my," said his wife from the shadows. The maid had returned, saying the shop was sold out of simmered beans, so she bought red miso and tofu. Tofu had gone up five rin, she said. Night worshippers were chanting away behind Sennenji temple. The wife's face again appeared from the other room.

"Dear?"

Dōya-sensei had closed his notebook and was now writing earnestly on fresh sheets of manuscript paper.

"Dear?!" his wife called the second time.

"What is it?"

"Dinner is ready."

"I'll be there in a minute."

Dōya-sensei met her glance for a moment and then returned to his desk. His wife's face soon disappeared. Suppressed laughter rose from the kitchen. Dōya was not disposed to taking dinner until he had finished the paragraph he was now writing. Finally finding a convenient place to leave off writing, he laid down his brush and looked at the pile of manuscript paper. Rifling through the pages, he said to himself, "Two hundred and thirty-one pages." Apparently he was engaged in writing a book.

He stood up and entered the next room. Over a small, oblong wooden brazier was boiling a pot of white tofu, steaming and trembling in the water.

"Boiled tofu?"

"Yes, I am sorry that is all we have."

"Quite all right. Anything will do, provided I don't starve," Dōya said and sat down at a small tray table and took up his chopsticks from a squarish box.

"Look at you! You are still wearing your split skirt trousers. That's a bit much," his wife said, serving him a bowl of rice.

"I have forgotten because I am very busy."

"You make yourself busy by your own choice," she said, replacing the pot with an iron kettle.

"You think so?" replied Dōya undisturbed by his wife's comment.

"Yes. You have declined all profitable jobs and have accepted the ones with too much work and too little income. Anybody would say that is eccentric of you."

"Let them think so then. It is a matter of principle with me."

"It is all very well for you to stand on your principles, but as for me . . ."

"You are saying you dislike principles?"

"It is not a matter of what I like or dislike. At least . . . I should like to be like most people."

"So long as we have enough to eat we should be content. Once one has developed a taste for luxuries, there is no end to it."

"You may be right. And I suspect you will not mind what may become of me."

"This miso is very salty. Where did you buy it?"

"I do not know."

Dōya-sensei raised his eyes and looked at the opposite wall. An enlarged shadow of his wife loomed on the grey chilly surface.

To his eyes both the wife and the shadow appeared to have equal insignificance.

Beside the shadow on the wall a woman's overcoat, in what appeared to be twisted silk yarn, was draped over a clothes stand. It looked a little too showy for his wife. But he remembered that he had bought it for her while they were living in the country and financial times were better. He had a different way of thinking then too: he supposed that there were more than a few people in the world who agreed with him in thought and sentiment. So he had not yet considered taking the lead in rousing people with the power of his pen.

Things were different now. The world sang the praises of aristocrats, the world sang the praises of the wealthy, the world even sang the praises of doctorates and baccalaureates. When they encountered a man of character, they did not know how to appreciate his value apart from his social position or wealth, education or talent. Their measure of man was not his character but his accessories. If character came to blows with accessories, the latter would be championed and the former trampled. The loss of a single man of character would be the loss of some of the light of the world, irreplaceable by a hundred aristocrats, a hundred millionaires, or a hundred doctorates. I was born into this world to uphold the value of character, Dōya thought to himself. Working for a living was merely a means to fulfill his mission. He ground his ink-stone and wielded his brush for no other purpose than to bring home to others the supreme value of character. This was Dōya's present conviction. Living solely for his convictions, Dōya could not afford to humor his wife.

After looking at the kimono on the wall for a while, Dōya finished his dinner. "Have you been somewhere today?" he asked.

"Yes," his wife answered bluntly. Dōya silently sipped his tea. Her reply was as quiet as autumn wind in withering grass.

His wife broached the topic: "It is impossible to postpone the repayment to Sanada indefinitely, and we must do something about what we owe to the landlord, and since I shall have to manage somehow to meet the bills for rice and firewood—I have been out trying to raise some money today."

"I see. Then you've been to the pawnbroker's?"

"We have nothing left to pawn," she said, looking reproachfully at her husband.

"Then where did you go?"

"I had no where else to go, so I paid to visit to your elder brother."

"My elder brother? It's no use going to him for help. What can we expect from him?"

"There you go abusing others from the start. I don't like it. Whatever difference in education or temperament there may be between you and him, he is still you blood brother, isn't he?"

"Yes we are brothers. I don't deny it."

"Oughtn't you take counsel of your own knees, as the saying goes? In such straits as we are in, you ought to go and consult with him, I should think."

"No, I will never go."

"That is being obstinate, your customary habit. Is it not unprofitable to want to make yourself disliked by others?"

Dōya fell silent, vacantly watching the moving shadow of his wife on the wall.

"Have you succeeded in raising money?"

"You always jump to conclusions, don't you?"

"What conclusions?"

"Well, there are various preliminaries and contrivances one needs to consider before going out to raise money, you know."

"I see. Then I will rephrase my question: I understand you visited my brother, did you not?—and in secret."

"In secret for your sake, it was."

"Fine. In secret for my sake. And then?"

"When I visited your brother, I first apologized for our long neglect to call on him. And after some small talk, I proceeded to disclose all our financial difficulties."

"And then what happened?"

"Then your brother was very sympathetic toward me and said he was sorry to find me in such hard circumstances."

"He sympathized, did he? Hmmm. Hand me that charcoal basket. The fire will go out unless it is fed with some fresh charcoal."

"And he said our money matters must be put in order without delay. He asked why we had let matters go on for so long."

"How indulgent of him."

"You still doubt your brother's sincerity, don't you? Some day Heaven will punish you for that."

"Did he offer to lend us some money, then?"

"There you are again—jumping to conclusions!"

Dōya-sensei felt amused at this, and bending down with a smile, began to blow on the charcoal.

"He asked how much would be needed to liquidate all our debts, but

I felt ashamed to mention the sum at first. Finally, I summoned the cour-age—." She broke off, while Dōya went on blowing on the charcoal.

"Please listen, dear. Finally, I summoned the courage—. Are you listen-ing to me?"

"I'm listening," he replied, raising his face, flushed with the heat of the glowing charcoal.

"Summoning courage, I said, 'One hundred yen.'"

"You must have given him quite a surprise."

"Then he said, 'One hundred yen is a considerable sum. It is not easy to raise so much money.'"

"Just what one might expect him to say."

"Please be patient and listen to the rest of my story! He said, 'Since this is an urgent matter,' he said, 'I personally will serve as guarantor and pro-cure a loan for you.'"

"I doubt that."

"Will you just please listen until I am finished?! He said further, howev-er, that he would see you about the matter, and after hearing your opinion, he would make a decision. You see how far I have pushed things along." The wife lifted up her high-cheek-boned face and looked as if she had achieved a great success. She watched her husband's face. Her look seemed to say that he was good for nothing, bent over his desk working ploddingly day and night, but not lifting a finger to support himself in comfort—or his wife.

"I see," was all he said. He made no attempt to express his gratitude for what her resourcefulness had accomplished.

"You disappoint me with your indifference. I have succeeded thus far. The rest depends on you. It is your turn to do something. If you mismanage, all my efforts will have been in vain."

"You needn't be so anxious. Within the next month I have prospects of coming into one or two hundred yen," Dōya-sensei declared flatly.

Dōya's fixed income amounted to twenty yen from his editorship of *The World* magazine and fifteen yen from his compilation of an English-Japanese dictionary. Apart from these, he toiled ceaselessly noon and night, contrib-uting articles to newspapers and magazines. None of this writing brought in any money. So he was surprised when remuneration of one or two yen trickled in.

These literary works of his, which bore no material rewards, were his life. His soul was transformed into each drop of ink, and every word was alive with his spirit. When Dōya wielded his brush even to write a fragment, he hoped that it would meet the reader's eye and produce a line of electric current that would tremble throughout the body of the reader. Each time he started on a fresh sheet of manuscript paper, he would swear anew his conviction that his brush was a sacred vehicle to convey the Way, and he would allow no one, not even God, to interfere with his mission. In the act of writing, he felt as if the fire of his enthusiasm would pass through his fingertips onto the paper so as to scorch it. If there is prose capable of converting a blank sheet of paper into an author's moral convictions, into sentences upsurging and drenched with sweat, that would be Dōya's writing. Unfortunately, the world belongs to aristocrats, to the wealthy, to doctorates, and to scholars. It is a world in which accessories prevail over the true value of man. Dōya's writings were ignored each time they were published. His wife called his unprofitable activity "writing as a hobby," and one who wrote as a hobby was a good-for-nothing.

Having listened to Dōya's prospects for future income, his wife stuck the tongs in the ashes and asked skeptically, "Is it really possible for you now to expect that kind of money to come in?"

"Are you saying my stock has depreciated since former days?" Dōya said, laughing out loud.

The wife, taken aback, opened wide her mouth.

"Well, back to my writing desk," said Dōya, standing up. That night he brought his manuscript, *An Essay on Character*, up to page two hundred and fifty. It was past two in the morning when he went to bed.

4

"Where are you going?" Nakano asked Takayanagi, apprehending him in front of the zoo at Ueno Park. The thick blackish trunks of the cherry trees reflected the autumn sunshine. The branches dropped their dying leaves, some of them falling onto the shoulders of people walking under the trees. Leaves littered the ground here and there.

The leaves were of various colors. Gazing at them, Takayanagi imagined that fresh blood exposed to the sun for a week and then painted on the backside of the leaves would result in this color. The association with blood caused Takayanagi to break out in a cold sweat. He gave an involuntary cough.

The leaves were of various shapes. Like dried rice cakes turning into myriad forms when toasted, each leaf curved and bowed in its own way. The fallen cherry leaves turned and twisted in the wind. Desiccated things, having no regrets, no attachments, blow where the winds of uncertainty may take them, twirling merrily in a dance of death. Whirling leaves and dust driven by the wind are a form of madness—only they are lifeless. The interspersion of death and madness into the world of nature by Takayanagi made him shrug his shoulders and give another hollow cough.

At this moment Nakano surprised Takayanagi. Coming to his senses, Takayanagi felt the world was serene. Under a bright sky, beautifully dressed people walked by one after another. Nakano was wearing a fine-fitting thin woolen overcoat and a gleaming pearl in his cravat. Takayanagi observed him silently.

"Where are you going?" the youth asked again.

"I have just been to the library," replied Takayanagi, breaking his silence at last.

"Still at work on *How to Teach Geography*, are you? Ha, ha, ha. You look gloomy. What is the matter?"

"I have recently dropped the comic half of my mask somewhere."

"And in search of it you went to the office beyond Shinbashi where you were mistreated, is that it? How deplorable."

"I would go in search for it not only to the office beyond Shinbashi but to the corners of the earth, but I shall never recover it. I give up."

"What are you giving up?"

"Everything!"

"You mean to say you'll give up everything? Perhaps you had better do so for the time being. Give up everything, but come with me now."

"Where?"

"A charity concert is to be given today, and I was obliged to buy two tickets. But no one else wanted to attend. Yet, here you are. So you must come with me."

"You buy tickets you cannot even use. A waste of money, I should say."

"It was an obligation. In fact, it was my father who bought them, but he does not appreciate Western music."

"Then you ought to have yielded the spare ticket."

"I thought of sending it to you."

"No, not to me, but to somebody else."

"Somebody else? Ah, I see you mean her. But I did not send it to her. She has her own ticket."

Takayanagi made no reply and looked the other party in the face. Nakano, smiling shyly, began to beat his coat lapels with a pair of kid gloves in his right hand.

"Why do you carry gloves in your hand instead of wearing them?"

"Well, I just took them out of my pocket," Nakano said, putting them back into an inside pocket. This seemed to calm the irritated nerves of his friend.

From behind they heard a carriage driver's "Hey!" and the sound of dashing horses' hooves. The two young men stepped aside quickly. A black landau with its top lowered because of the warm autumn sun passed by carrying one silk hat and one pretty red parasol.

"Those are the kind attending the concert?" Takayanagi asked, indicating the receding vehicle with his chin.

"That was Marquis Tokugawa," Nakano explained.

"In the know, aren't you? Are you a retainer of the Marquis?"

"No, I am not," Nakano riposted, with a serious face. Takayanagi felt secretly pleased.

"Now let us go, otherwise we shall be late for the concert."

"If we are late you mean you will not be able to see her."

Nakano blushed slightly. Whether it was because he was angry, or because his pretext was seen through, or because he was ashamed, none could tell except Takayanagi.

"In any event, let us go. Your utter dislike of crowded places will result in your becoming a loner."

Those who give a blow must receive a blow. Now it was Takayanagi's turn to suffer a hit. When he heard the word "loner, " he felt his ears tingle and realized his own solitariness.

"You won't come? If you are disinclined to go, I cannot help it. I must say good-bye." As his friend turned on his heels, smiling a smile of pity,

Takayanagi received another blow.

"Let's go," he said, simply yielding to the proposal. This was his first experience attending a concert.

When they arrived at the entrance, the reception desk was so busy directing people to the left and right that the blue-ribbon badges of the ushers were lost in the crowd. First-class ticket holders were to go to the right and second-class to the left. There were no third-class seats. Nakano, of course, had first-class tickets, and, turning around to Takayangi, said, "Come this way," like a man thoroughly at home in his environment. Ascending the staircase and following Nakano's lead, the solitary young man thought to himself that if it were possible he would like to have an extra seat provided in third class for him to listen to the music today. He felt as if those ascending the staircase with him on either side and those following like a herd from behind were animals of a different stripe, deliberately closing in on him and forcing him upward into the spacious hall upstairs, only to mock him by clapping their hands and laughing at him. Looking back, he saw the tops of female heads in raven tresses and male heads with hair parted neatly in a seven to three ratio and smoothed into place by pomade. Below him were ten to twenty more heads coming up from behind so as to make it impossible for Takayanagi Shūsaku to retreat a single step.

Upon entering the concert hall, he found himself in a haze, as if in a drunken stupor. He felt like a mountain-climber, who, after trudging through dense underbrush completely shutting out the sky, suddenly reaches the summit and looks down on a boundless view of the country below. The stage was far down in the bottom of the valley. To get there, one would have to descend by way of the precisely divided lines between the tiers of people till he reached the bottom floor of the hall. The floor formed a semi-circle, parallel to which rose half-rings of human walls one above the other till they nearly reached the ceiling. Going down seven or eight steps, Takayanagi happened to look up to the rows rising to the ceiling and, feeling slightly giddy, had to stop for a moment. "Excuse me," a large foreigner said in English, overshadowing Takayanagi, and stepping down to the next tier. An ostrich feather swept by his nose and the whiff of an elegant scent of perfume wafted pass him. A big bald-headed man carefully carrying a silk hat, who passed by the two young men sideways, followed her.

"Look! There are two vacant seats," said Nakano in his element, cutting through a row of seats. The people sitting in the row stood up to let them pass. "If I were alone," thought Takayanagi, "no one would take the trouble to rise for me."

"What a crowd!" said Nakano, taking his seat and surveying the entire hall. Then he noticed his friend's appearance and whispered to him, "I say. You must take off your hat."

Takayanagi quickly removed his hat and looked left and right. Finding three or four pairs of eyes fixed on his head, he felt besieged by an alien army. Naturally, he was the only person in the entire hall who had left his hat on.

"May I leave my overcoat on?" asked Takayanagi.

"Yes, you may. But since it is too warm, I will take mine off," Nakano said and stood up. Quickly turning the collar inside out three inches, he slipped off his left sleeve; as he was slipping off his right sleeve, he caught hold of the collar and, turning the coat inside out, folded it and placed it over the back of the seat. Underneath he wore a new frock coat and a waistcoat with the lapels trimmed in white in the latest fashion. Takayanagi looked on his friend's dexterity with admiration. Nakano did not sit down again, but remained standing with one hand on the back of the seat and looked about in all directions. Many eyes converged on him, but he was undisturbed. Takayanagi regarded his calmness with envy.

Out of a thousand faces in the audience, Nakano seemed to find the one he was seeking, his cheeks radiated charm, and he nodded at her. Takayanagi could not help but look in the same direction. To find where his friend's greeting was extended, he slyly turned his head, and, looking up three rows at an angle, his eyes fell on her. He saw a young lady straightening her slender neck after bowing, raising her black hair decorated with a largish yellow ribbon fluttering like a butterfly. There was a faint blush on her cheeks, and, shaded by long, moist-looking lashes, her eyes, drawing one into the world of dreams, were fixed in the direction of Nakano. Takayanagi was entranced.

His split skirt was of dark cotton weave, his overcoat was faded, and the accumulated grime was conspicuously shiny in the sun. He hadn't had a bath in days, and his shirt needed washing. He and the concert were completely incompatible. As for him and his friend?—They were no more compatible. His high-collar friend and the owner of those enchanting eyes could commune by a wireless electric energy, even if separated by a thousand miles. How much more so now that they were thrown together in the fragrant and genial atmosphere of the present hall. Their souls would melt and flow toward each other, coming together and vibrating like the strings of a harp. The thousands of concertgoers seemed to welcome these two handsome young people with open arms, while rejecting Takayanagi by thumbing their noses at him. He regretted that he had ever come to a place like this. But his friend was unaware of it.

"It's time. They will soon begin!" said Nakano, looking at his printed program.

"Oh?" said Takayanagi, looking mechanically at his own copy. The program stated: *I. Violin, cello, piano ensemble.* He did not know what a cello was. *II. Sonata . . . by Beethoven.* He knew the name of the composer and nothing else. *III. Adagio . . . by Perger.* He knew nothing of this item. Coming to *IV,* he was startled by thunderous applause. The performers had already appeared on stage.

Soon the performance by the trio began. All the audience fell silent as if fossilized. From one of the right-hand windows one could see the upper half of a fir tree, and beyond it the country of sky. Through the green curtains at one of the left-hand windows, the sunshine of a transparent autumn day shone through obliquely onto the white wall.

The music was proceeding pleasantly in the environment of silent nature and silent audience. The opulent sound coursed through the air into Nakano's eardrums, and he was pleased to discover that different tones had their own colors, while Takayangi watched a kite circling above the fir trees. He fancied that the bird was flying in tune to the music, and he wondered at his own conceit.

A loud clapping of hands brought Takayanagi to his senses. He found that he was once again a solitary individual amid animals of a different stripe. At his side, his friend clapped enthusiastically. His friend was one of those calling him back, forcing him to return from the towering heights of the kite in flight to the narrow valley of the hall.

The second item of the program followed. The audience became breathless at once. Takayanagi felt at ease once more. He looked out the window but could see the kite no longer. His eyes traveled to the ceiling where he found three beams about one foot in circumference and hexagonal in shape running the length of the concert hall. But where they ended he could not tell, unless he twisted his neck to see. The beams were decorated with a design of intertwined flowers and vines. Looking up at them he felt as if he were in a large Buddhist temple. Yellow-colored voices and blue-colored voices seemed to entwine like the painted vines and to fall down on his ears. Takayanagi felt as if he were alone on a deserted island.

Applause broke out for the third time. His friend at his side clapped his hands more furiously than the rest. The solitary man stranded on a deserted island felt as if hailstones were pounding him. The barrage continued. As the musician was about to disappear off stage, the applause increased in intensity. Carrying her violin warmly under her right arm, she turned toward the audience, stirring up her kimono skirt with a maple-leaf pattern in subdued tones. In her outstretched sleeve she received a bouquet of white chrysanthemums bursting in bloom, and she slightly inclined the upper half of her body toward the audience. Takayanagi then felt that he had heard her music not as a member of the audience but as one who forbidden to hear, had to steal up to her and eavesdrop.

Before the applause had quite died down, the next piece began. In an instant the audience became silent as the grave. Takayanagi felt liberated again. He felt as if he were standing alone on a sweeping plain, watching a hot sun, red like an overripe persimmon, rising on the horizon. As a child, he had frequently had this feeling. Why did he now find himself constrained, spurned by people on every side? Even his only friend clapped his hands horribly at critical moments. When one has no one to turn to, one must return to one's parents, as the saying goes. Takayanagi thought to himself that, if he had parents to return to, he should not have become what he was. When Takayanagi was six years old, his father went away and never came back. After that, his friends ceased to play with him. He asked his mother what happened to Father, and she replied each time, "He'll be back. He'll be back." She put off her boy with false hopes, knowing full well that his father would never return. His mother was still alive. She had disposed of the house where they had lived for so many years, moved to a mountain village six miles away from his native town, and was living a lonely life there. Now that he had graduated, he ought to have her come to Tokyo to live with him, as a dutiful son should do, provided he had a good job. If, according to the saying, he should return to his parent, there would be nothing to expect but for mother and son to starve to death. At this moment, applause burst forth from the audience.

"That was delightful! It was the best so far. The musician could really bring out the spirit of the piece. What did you think?" Nakano asked.

"Hmmm."

"Did you not find it delightful?"

"Yes, very."

"Your response is disappointing. —Look! There, beside the European, the woman wearing the small-patterned Yuzen kimono. That kind of pattern is in vogue nowadays. Is it not gorgeous?"

"I suppose so."

"Have you no sense of color? Such a gorgeous ensemble is superbly suited to occasions such as these. Seen from afar, its attractiveness does not pale. Exquisite!"

"Your betrothed is also dressed like that, I see."

"Is that so? If she is, she just happens to be dressed so."

"'Just happens to be dressed so' sounds like an excuse for being attractively dressed."

Nakano broke off the conversation for a while. To their left a man in pince-nez with his hair shaved close on the sides of his head, wrote busily in a notebook.

"Is that man a music critic?" asked Takayanagi this time.

"Who? That man in black? No, he is a portrait artist. He comes regularly, and every time he brings his sketchbook with him to sketch people's faces."

"Without his subjects' permission?"

"Well, yes."

"Then he is a thief. A face thief."

Nakano chuckled. There was a ten-minute intermission. Takayanagi observed people going out into the corridor, others going into the smoking-room, still others returning to their seats from the bathrooms. The women were so pretty they reminded him of his childhood experience of leafing through Toyokuni's color prints of *Rustic Genji*. The men seemed as if they had come alive from Yoshitoshi's prints of the *Forty-Seven Rōnin*. But when Takayanagi reflected on how he himself might appear in their eyes, he wanted to leave at once. All around him was abuzz with activity. But these people were not active for the sake of earning a living; they were actively engaged in the pursuit of pleasure. Like butterflies fluttering in the flowers or waterweeds swaying in the ripples, their activity was above practical purposes. People who entered this hall must be those whose needs rose above the practical business of life.

Takayanagi's activities, on the other hand, were wholly concerned with earning his daily bread. They were not pleasant like a spring breeze, but stern like the withering late autumn gale. He had to work ceaselessly to expiate his sin of being born unconditionally into this world. Rationally speaking, he had no reason to feel ashamed when compared to present company who enjoyed themselves like sportive butterflies. His silence was not because he had nothing to say; on the contrary, he had important things to say: words that would make people nod in agreement, words that people would cling to. All his time was taken up with the struggle to live; he could not afford to give utterance to them. He could not say what he wanted to say, the world could not listen even if it wanted to listen, because his hands were bound by fate and his mouth was gagged by society. Had he been given a fortune of millions on the condition that he not spend a single cent of it, he would have been unable to recover his former contentment with poverty and would curse his cruel fate. Was he going to die cursing his own fate?—Here he choked up and had a fit of coughing. Taking a handkerchief from his pocket, he wiped away the phlegm, noticing that the white cloth had turned disgustingly brown. Looking up he saw a lady with a thin gold chain around her neck, which was attached to a watch hidden inside her vermilion and yellow sash. She was standing at the end of his row of seats and greeting Nakano.

"I am so glad you have come," she said, narrowing her lovely double-lidded eyes.

"The concert is a great success, is it not? Fuyuta-san's performance was splendid," Nakano replied, half turning to her.

"Yes, I was thrilled," she said in parting, and descended the steps.

"You know her, do you?" asked Nakano.

"How would I know her?" Takayanagi said, snubbing his friend.

Nakano was surprised into silence. At that moment the second half of the program began. The piece was called "Where the Four-Leaf Clovers Grow." Takayanagi listened drowsily. At the sound of clapping he returned to his senses like a man awakening from a feverish dream. After two or three repetitions of this process, he was finally awakened from his illusions by the beating of cymbals and the sounding of horns in a march from *Tannhäuser*.

Soon an audience of over a thousand began to move at once. The two young men went out the gate, jostled by the crowd. Night was falling. The pine grove at the side of the library gradually deepened from barely perceptible green to black.

"It is getting chilly."

Takayanagi's response was two lifeless coughs.

"I notice you have been coughing. It sounds strange. You should see a doctor about it."

"It's nothing, really," replied Takayanagi, shrugging his bony shoulders two or three times.

Traversing the pine grove, they came out in front of the museum. In a tall gingko tree a number of crows, like so many ink spots, were stirring about and getting ready to roost for the night. Fallen leaves glowed in the dusky air. A wind had sprung up.

"Two or three days ago I received a visit from a man called Shirai Dōya."

"Dōya-sensei?!"

"I believe so. It is an unusual name."

"Did you ask him?"

"I wanted to ask him, but it was too awkward."

"Why?"

"Well, I could not say, 'Are you the teacher who was driven away by his middle school students?' now could I?"

"You need not have asked in such a blunt way."

"He is not a man easily questioned. There is something disquieting about him. He will say nothing apart from his business."

"Perhaps he has turned into such a man. But on what business was he calling?"

"As an editor of *The World* magazine, he came to interview me."

"An interview? Well, the world seems to be taking a queer course. Money, I see, is the ruling force after all."

"Why?"

"Well. —I am sorry he has fallen so low. —How was he dressed?"

"He was not very well dressed."

38

"If not well dressed, what was the condition of his dress?"

"It is difficult to say. But if you insist, he was as well dressed as you are."

"As well dressed as I? Then was his overcoat as old as this?"

"It was not so faded in color."

"What about his split skirt trousers?"

"His divided skirt was not of cotton, but it was severely wrinkled."

"Then he was no better dressed or worse dressed than I."

"Yes, neither better nor worse dressed."

"I see. —He is a remarkably tall and slender man. Did you find him so?"

"Yes, a tall man with a long face."

"Then I am certain it was Dōya-sensei. —This is a hard-hearted world, indeed. —You remember his address, don't you?"

"I did not ask his address."

"You didn't?"

"No. But you can find out from the magazine office. He may be involved with other magazines and newspapers as well. I seem to have seen the name Dōya somewhere."

The two young men were outstripped by carriages and ricksha hurrying home from the concert in rapid succession. Two other ricksha came rapidly from behind them, but instead of passing them, turned at the corner of the grounds of the Great Bronze Buddha toward the Seiyōken restaurant, the drivers shouting gallantly. The women riding in them were so splendidly dressed as to spark attention even despite the whitish mist and the gathering dusk. Nakano stopped short and said, "I must be going now. I have an engagement."

"A dinner engagement at Seiyōken restaurant, by any chance?"

"Yes it is. Goodbye," answered Nakano, and he began walking toward the restaurant, leaving Takayangi alone in the middle of the road.

Feeling anew his solitariness in the world, he went down to the edge of the pond. The solitary Shūsaku thought to himself, "If I had time for a love affair, I would write of my own agonizing experiences in a novel and have it published." Looking up, he saw the gas-flame lights flickering in the upstairs rooms of the restaurant.

5

Takayanagi entered a milk bar. He sat down in a chair by a papered sliding door that had frosted glass panes above and below. He had toast and a glass of milk. In his purse he had twenty yen, fifty sen, which he had just received in exchange for forty-one manuscript pages of his translation *How to Teach Geography*. Fifty sen a page was the rate. The terms were that remuneration was not to exceed fifty sen a page, and the monthly amount of translation was not to exceed fifty pages.

He hoped that he could manage to live on the money for the present month. From another source he expected ten yen, but he had earmarked it for his mother in his native province. He remembered that it was the season for catching *ayu* sweet-fish coming downstream in his province. Possibly the first frost of the season was whitening the thatched roof of his mother's ramshackle house, and the chickens were devastating the roots of the chrysanthemums. Was his mother keeping well?

Opposite him two students monopolized a whole table for themselves. They were hotly debating the box-office revenues of the chrysanthemum doll show at Dangozaka while eating Western cakes. To the left, a lone student peeled a mandarin orange and squeezed its juice into a glass of milk. After each squeeze he turned a page of geisha photographs in *Literary Club* magazine, another squeeze of the orange, another turn of the page. When he came to the end of the geisha pictures, he stirred the contents of his glass with a spoon and made a curious face. He was surprised to find his milk curdled by the addition of the orange acid.

Takayanagi pulled out some magazines from under a pile of newspapers and glanced through them. The magazine he was searching for, *The World*, was folded under a copy of the *Asahi Shinbun*. Though folded back, it was still new, having just come out four or five days before. The pages at which it was folded back were printed in no. 6 type and heavily underscored in colored pencil. Under the title, "My View of Romantic Love," was the name Nakano Shuntai. Shuntai was a pen name for Kiichi. Leaving his half-eaten toast on his plate, Takayanagi read the article and smiled a sardonic smile. At the end of the article someone had written in the same colored pencil the word "Erotomaniac!!!" Takayanagi turned the page. The column in small type was extensive, containing contributions from various people. At the very beginning was an article "On Today's Anguished Youth," as construed by numerous authors. Takayanagi felt a sudden impulse to read on. The first one advised youth to cultivate mental quietude. He found no hint of a suggestion as to how mental quietude could be cultivated. The second one urged the taking of exercise and cold-water massages. Too simplistic, thought Takayanagi. The third one argued that youth who read no books and lacked experience in life had no cause for anguish. They may have no cause, thought Takayanagi, but the fact of anguish was undeniable. The fourth one suggested that students should travel during each school vacation. No suggestion was made, however, as to sources of travel funding, thought Takayanagi. By this time he had grown tired of reading. Turning back the pages, he came to page one, where he found an essay, "Attachment and Emancipation," signed by "Yūseishi, A Social Critic." The title piqued his curiosity enough for him to glance over it.

When something is wrong with a certain part of your body, you cannot help but worry about it. Whatever you may be engaged in, you will fixate on that ailing part of your body. A person in perfect health, on the other hand, is never aware of the existence of his own body. His mind is at ease because he has no part of his body on which to focus unnecessary attention. Once, on seeing a pale-looking, thin man, I inquired as to the condition of his stomach. He replied, "There is nothing wrong with my stomach. As proof I can say that I've lived to this age and still don't know where my stomach is." I laughed at his remark but later realized that they were enlightened words. His stomach was in perfect working order so he had no reason to be concerned about it, even being indifferent to its location. He might eat and drink with impunity whatever he liked. He was enlightened so far as his stomach was concerned.

"This is a little strange," Takayanagi muttered to himself, "being enlightened about one's stomach."

What may be said about the stomach may be said about the whole body; what may be said about the whole body may be said about the mind. As regards the mind, however, it is more likely than the body to cause trouble because it is not exempt from attachment to either advantages or disadvantages.

One who excels in an art or profession is always conscious of his advantage, and this consciousness sometimes proves troublesome. One may transcend the ever-present consciousness of his own art or profession, but one is not easily emancipated from the consciousness of his own disadvantages.

When a women goes to a concert wearing an obi worth a hundred or two hundred yen, she will be distracted by the costly article and unable to enjoy the music—all because she is attached to the obi. But this is an example of pride. It is easier to escape the evils of pride than the strong emotions associated with disgrace. A long time ago, when I was introduced to a fellow guest at a certain house, we both bowed to each other while remaining seated, and, while looking down, I noticed he had a hole in his sock, revealing his big toe. I looked away, and he quickly covered his torn sock with his other foot. This man was fixated on the hole in his sock. . . .

"I'm fixated too," thought Takayanagi, "my whole body is riddled with holes." He read on.

Enslavement of the mind is painful. It must be avoided. In this world it is impossible to avoid all pain. The pain of an enslaved mind lasts for five or six days, extending way beyond the pain that subsides in a day. This form of pain is unnecessary. It must be avoided.

One's persistent fixation on his own defects is due to the awareness that others will notice—because others are fixated as well. . . .

Takayanagi recollected his own experience at today's concert.

Consequently, there are two ways to be emancipated from such attachment. One way is not to fixate no matter how much others fixate on your defects. You must carry on with what you are doing, remaining entirely indifferent, however hard they may look at you, however eagerly they may listen to you, however sharply they may criticize you, or however loudly they may rebuke you. Remember the anecdote of Ōkubo Hikozaemon going to Edo Castle, riding in a washtub to have an audience with the Shogun. . . .

Takayanagi felt envious of Hikozaemon.

A packhorse driver bedecked in splendid attire will at once become self-conscious, just as a nobleman or daimyo will become self-conscious if made to wear a packhorse driver's work apron. In this respect, Sakyamuni and Confucius were emancipated. Those who attach no importance to the things of this world have no reason to be disturbed by them. . . .

Takayanagi gulped down his tepid milk and uttered a deep sound.

The second way of emancipation is what ordinary people adopt. Their way is not to free themselves from attachments but rather to avoid placing themselves in situations that require emancipation. It is to take care from the beginning not to invite the pain caused by attracting another's notice of one's own behavior. So if one is not prepared to comply with the fashions of the time and flatter the world, one can hardly succeed in becoming emancipated. The merchant class of Edo practiced this way of emancipation. Geisha and men-about-town practiced it. Gentlemen in Europe practice it most punctiliously.

Thinking it interesting that geisha and gentlemen should be put together in the same class, Takayanagi bit off a corner of his toast and wiped his butter-smeared thumb on the knee of his split skirt trousers.

From the point of view of geisha, gentlemen, and men-about-town—Jesus, Confucius, and Sakyamuni are perfect mad men. From the point of view of Jesus, Confucius, and Sakyamuni, however, geisha, gentlemen, and men-about-town have yet to be emancipated, for while still enslaved, they merely fancy themselves free. The principles underlying both forms of emancipation are incompatible.

Takayanagi had never before thought about the word emancipation. Hitherto, his mind had been completely taken up with the thought that though he wanted to become somebody in the world of literature, his ambition had been diminished, not because of his lack of genius, but because of his lack of time and money. Moreover, in his view, the world was persecuting him, and his whole mind was filled with indignation. He wanted to read the rest of the article.

Emancipation is nothing more than an expedient means. When in this degenerate world one has truth to proclaim, good to champion, beauty to espouse, emancipation is required as an expedient means to avoid entanglement in the world, to galvanize one's will to push forward, and to evade the pain of persecution by the foolish multitude. If a gifted man fails to achieve this means, he will fall into moral slavery and be no better than geisha, gentlemen, and men-about-town. It would be a matter of great regret for the good of society.

Emancipation is an expedient means. Whether the action, behavior, or discourse of one who has entered the gate of expedient means is right or wrong has nothing to do with emancipation. Therefore, we must cultivate taste with an aim that is true before we attain emancipation. If a man of learning should freely disseminate inferior taste, he would discredit himself. It is not for food, clothing, and shelter, not for fame or rank or wealth that the man of learning devotes ten or twenty years of his valuable time to the study of old books, but rather through his modest writings to light a torch illuminating the way through the gate of emancipation and enlighten the darkness of the world.

What enables those who have gained insight into the Way to rid themselves of enslavement and to approach the first order of emancipation is called morality. Morality is another word for the freedom obtainable to the believer of the Way so as to live in accordance with the Way. Those who do not understand this great morality are called vulgar people.

The vulgar form a vast majority of any society. They cannot understand the great morality because they are attached to their high positions in society; they cannot understand the great morality because they are attached to their riches; they, the inferior, cannot understand the great morality because they are attached to wine or women.

Light must precede taste. Taste is the lubricant for the machinery of society, without which the machinery would grind to a halt. With impure oil, it will become depraved. Gentlemen, men-about-town, and geisha are those who waste their lives, lubricated with impure oil. Aristocrats, politicians, and the wealthy seek to run the machinery of society in reverse with the oil of pedigree, the oil of political power, and the oil of monetary power.

They have no knowledge of genuine oil, for they have never studied what it is. Having never considered what it is, they may be excused for their failure to understand the great morality. But when they dare to persecute the seekers and followers of the light, they leave the flock of the vulgar and join the herd of the sinner.

It takes five or six years to learn how to play the samisen; in a month of study a learner still cannot distinguish a good musician from a bad one. It is absurd to think that the cultivation of taste is easier than learning how to play the samisen. Students of the tea ceremony do not resent spending their precious time practicing useless etiquette, implicitly obeying every instruction of the tea master. Taste is a more difficult matter than the tea ceremony. If they are modest enough to respect a tea master, how much more worthy of respect are the teachings of the man of learning, for whom taste is his object of study.

Taste is important to mankind. If one should destroy all musical instruments, he would be a sinner in depriving society of music. If one should burn all books, he would be a sinner in depriving the world of learning. If one should corrupt taste itself, he would be a terrible sinner, worse than a convicted criminal, because he destroys society. We can live without music. We can live without learning. Taste, however, is an essential element of society that pervades all aspects of life. Trying to live without it is to inhabit a wilderness of tigers.

Here is a man. He cannot become the man he desires to become because many will persecute him day and night, finally succeeding in the course of time in degrading his character and debasing his taste. They will have committed a crime graver than murder. If you take a human life, your life will be taken. A murderer is executed and disappears from society, leaving no evil behind. But he who has debased the taste of another, yet survives in the world, will infect others with corrupt taste. He is like a plague, and those who have introduced a plague are of course the great sinners against society.

Those who cast a pestilence on the world of taste and go unpunished for it are like murderers who escape their due punishment. Those who rank high in society are most likely to commit this sin. Due to their high social position, they are capable of exerting strong influence over others. If they do not know how to use their influence properly, they are dangerous people.

In matters of taste, they are inferior to the scholars who specialize in the problem; yet they have greater influence than such scholars. Capability is not power. Some of the influential do not even understand the distinction between capability and power. They try to twist men of letters around their fingers, men whose mission it is to educate the world about taste. Not only have they forgotten the great morality, but in committing the great immorality they ride roughshod over members of society.

The scholar who allows his will to be bent by the influential has no self-awareness of his own high mission. The scholar who cannot educate them is a cowardly scholar. The scholar seeks to advance toward the light and exerts himself to promote the idea of taste according to the light. In promoting the idea of taste according to the light, he seeks to evade attachment. In evading attachment, he seeks emancipation.

Leaving the magazine opened at this page, Takayanagi raised his eyes in a dazed state. An octagonal-shaped clock on a pillar near the entrance chimed one o'clock. A waitress sitting under the clock suddenly stood up. On a round table stood a cheap vase of Kyoto porcelain containing some narcissus, the tips of the leaves turning yellow and looking like they needed watering. The waitress touched the flowers and then picked up a newspaper

44

lying next to the vase. Instead of reading it, she folded it twice and laid it aside. She had stood up with no particular business to attend to. Out of boredom she had mechanically started up at the chime of the clock. Takayanagi envied her.

The two students were smoking now, looking vacantly into the street; they seemed to have finished their discussion of the chrysanthemum-doll show revenue.

"Look! There goes Tomita!" one of them exclaimed.

"Where?" asked the other. Tomita was seen for a moment through a three-inch gap in the glass doors.

"There goes a real glutton!"

"He never stops eating," which seemed to prove that Tomita was no ordinary glutton.

"People do not get fat in proportion to the quantity of food they eat. Tomita eats like a pig but he never gains weight."

"In the same way that a man can read lots of books and never amount to something."

"Quite right. So we should do our best not to study too much."

"Ha, ha, ha! That is not what I meant."

"But that is precisely what *I* meant."

"Tomita does not get fat, but he is quick-witted. He may owe it to the large amount of food he consumes."

"In what way is he quick-witted?"

"Oh, when I was walking along Fourth Street someone called me from behind, and on looking back, I saw that it was Tomita. He had his hair only half cut and wore a cloth wrapped about his shoulders."

"What was the matter with him?"

"He had just flown out of a barber shop."

"But why?"

"Getting his hair cut, he happened to see my reflection in the barber's mirror and came out to see me."

"Ha, ha, ha. He must have been surprised to see you."

"I was surprised to see *him*. He forced me into donating to the Old Folk's Fund, and then returned to the barber shop."

"Ha, ha, ha! Now I see how clever he is. Now let us eat as much as possible! We must be clever or we shall find ourselves in difficulties after graduation."

"That's right. If we should be unable to earn twenty yen a month and continue to live in a boarding house like so many other graduates from the Literature Department, we shall find life hardly worth living."

Takayanagi paid his bill and stood up. When the waitress said "Thank you," the other student, who was dozing with his face in *Literary Club* magazine, looked up and gave Takayanagi an angry look with his sleepy, blood-shot eyes. The orange acid in his glass of milk must have poisoned him.

.

6

"Takayanagi Shūsaku is my name," he said, bowing his head respectfully. In the past he had bowed his head respectfully many times, but he had never done so from his heart as on this occasion. Whenever he visited a professor's house, or met with the man who gave him translation work, or saw any of his seniors, he never failed to bow respectfully. Just the other day when he was introduced to Nakano's father, he bowed most ceremoniously. On such occasions, however, he always felt overwhelmed by their social standing, greater age, fine dress, or glare of their residence, which seemed irresistibly to urge him to make an obeisance. But the effect from Dōya-sensei was completely different. His clothes were no better nor worse than Takayanagi's, as Nakano had described them. Sensei's study, like his own, also served as a parlor. Sensei's desk was of plain wood, uncovered and tastelessly squarish, as was his own. Sensei was pale and lean, as he was. In all these respects, Sensei was neither better nor worse than Takayanagi, yet the latter bowed respectfully, not because he was urged to do so by external circumstances, but because he preferred to do so, though he might have been less formal. His bow was a genuine expression of his love for a fellow creature. Wanting to reject all hypocritical obeisance in the world wherein one outwardly bowed politely while inwardly thinking "You bastard!" he bowed his head all the more deeply. Whether Dōya-sensei perceived all the meaning of his bow, he did not know.

"How do you do? I am Dōya Shirai," he said in an unaffected manner, which pleased Takayanagi very much. They remained silent for a while. Since Dōya did not know what brought his guest, he waited for him to announce his business. Takayanagi wanted to explain the former relationship between them so as to establish quickly a feeling of mutual sympathy, but the abruptness of his visit prevented his doing so. He could not speak, thinking that not so long ago his middle-school teacher, whom he together with other boys had driven to resign, might have fallen into this present poverty as a consequence. Under the circumstances, Takayanagi felt poorly lacking in boldness. On this visit he had intended to offer an apology, but, confronted with his old teacher, he felt too afraid to make amends for past sins. In his mind he created several opening phrases, but none seemed appropriate.

"It is getting chilly," Dōya-sensei said, making an impersonal remark about the weather, because he could not guess Takayanagi's thoughts.

"Yes, it has become quite chilly." Takayanagi's attempt to break the ice was completely frustrated by these words. He felt inclined to postpone his confession to the next visit. At the same time, he wanted to speak out.

"Are you busy, Sensei?"

"Yes, I am so busy I am worn thin. 'A poor man has no time to call his own' as they say."

Takayanagi's second attempt proved a failure. He wanted to start over.

"I have come to hear your opinion."

"Ah, an interview of some sort which you wish to publish in some magazine or other?"

Takayanagi again missed the mark. He was vexed that Sensei could not sense the earnestness of his attitude.

"No, that is not the case. Only . . . excuse me. —I did not mean to disturb you. Shall I call again at a more convenient time?"

"No, I am not at all bothered. I ask only because you spoke of hearing my opinion. No one, by the way, comes for my opinion."

"Oh, yes," the youth said, contradicting Sensei's statement in a strange way.

"What are you researching, if I may ask?"

"My research—. I have only just graduated this year."

"I see."

"Then what will you be working on?"

"I have much to work on, if I could. But I have no leisure time. . . . "

"It is not you alone that has no leisure, but I also. Perhaps it is better to have no leisure. You see, there are any number of people of leisure, yet hardly any of them actually produce any thing."

"But surely it depends on the person," Takayanagi said, hinting that if he had sufficient leisure, he would produce something.

"Yes, it may depend on the person. But as far as it concerns rich people . . ." Dōya broke off, and looked at something on his desk. There was a pile of manuscripts about two inches high. On the shoji door was cast the shadow of socks hanging to dry.

"No, the rich are no good. But those who suffer from lack of money . . ."

"Those who suffer from lack of money must make do as best they can," said Dōya-sensei calmly, though he himself was one such sufferer. Takayanagi was mildly dissatisfied with this argument.

"But if all their energy is spent earning a livelihood . . ."

"That is all right. If all their energy is exhausted by earning a living, then they need do nothing else."

The youth looked in bewilderment at Dōya, who was as perfectly sincere as Confucius. He could not brook ridicule, for he was by nature highly sensitive to ridicule, suspecting it in people's words where they did not intend it.

"That may be fine for you," Takayanagi said glibly, before he was aware of it. But no sooner had he said it than he realized the impropriety of his remark and looked down. But Dōya was unfazed.

"Of course I shall be satisfied with myself. As you should be also," he said, trying to include the other party.

"But why?" asked Takayanagi, like a frightened fox that runs away and then halts only to look back.

"Why? Did you not say you studied literature? Well, then?"

"Oh, yes. I have," Takayanagi replied emphatically. Although he could not answer any questions affirmatively, he would aver to anyone when his own territory was at stake.

"Then you ought to be satisfied with yourself too. Yes, you ought to be," Dōya-sensei repeated. But Takayanagi could not at all understand him. Yet he did not dare to ask for an explanation for fear of falling into an ambush. At a loss for what to do, he remained silent, watching Dōya's face, and hoping Dōya would resolve the situation. His gaze implied an urge for some move or other on the part of Dōya.

"Do you understand?" asked Dōya-sensei, which showed that Takayanagi's inquiring look had proven ineffective.

"Not exactly," he confessed.

"Don't you see? Literature is essentially different from other fields of study," Dōya-sensei said authoritatively.

"Ah," said Takayanagi unconsciously.

"As for other fields of study, obstacles to them and their research are the enemy. For example, poverty, busyness, pressure, misfortune, calamities, and so forth, all are enemies to those studies. Such things will hinder students from their research. These obstacles are to be avoided if students want to preserve their peace of mind and their leisure. In the past, men of letters have shared this opinion toward their study. It is thought that, of all professions, letters should be the least concerned with mundane affairs. Strange to say, men of letters themselves agree with the world on this view. But this is entirely wrong. Literature is life itself. Pain, poverty, sorrow—all events and conditions in life are the substance of literature, and those who have been able to savor these experiences are qualified men of letters. They are not men of leisure who can afford to wrack their brains over manuscript paper on their desks, searching for fine phrases with the help of a thesaurus. Provided we are possessed of a sense of taste that is ripe and rich and can navigate life's vicissitudes with the courage and sensitivity beyond the ordinary man, we are men of letters in the true sense of the term. When such navigation of life's vicissitudes is transferred to paper, they become literary works. Therefore, it is not a matter of reading books but of engaging life experiences that makes one a qualified man of letters. Consequently, those who pursue other fields of learning will do well to avoid hindrances to their research, staying aloof from a lived life, whereas men of letters must go forward to meet head-on the same obstacles."

"I see," Takayanagi said, looking queer.

"Don't you think so?"

Whether he had entertained such a notion before was beside the point when he had just heard it for the first time. For one can only give comments on such subjects as one has given consideration. An unexpected attack that can be overcome successfully ceases to be unexpected.

"Hmmm," Takayanagi said and hung his head. Though he had made literature his life, his view of it could not be very sound if he was at a loss to respond to others' opinions on the subject. If Dōya-sensei could hold these noble views on life and literature while living in such a humble house and wearing such shabby clothes, he should be content with a monthly income of twenty yen and fifty sen, he thought. He felt suddenly pulled into a wider world.

"Sensei, you seem to be very busy."

"Yes, I have thrown myself into a busy occupation by choice. In others' eyes I must appear an eccentric drudge. Ha, ha, ha!" For such a man, drudgery would cease to be drudgery.

"Excuse me, but in what work are you presently engaged?"

"Well, I am engaged in various work. I try to work for a living and work in my own area of interest. It's exhausting. Recently I was asked to interview some people for a magazine."

"You must find it very troublesome."

"One might call it troublesome. I call it farcical. But I generally manage to come away with some notes."

"You must hear some interesting things," Takayanagi said, trying to steer the conversation toward Nakano Shuntai.

"Oh, yes. The other day I had to listen to a lecture on *uma-uma*."

"*Uma-uma*?"

"Yes, you know, baby talk for 'food.' The etymology of *uma-uma*. According to the man's theory, the first sound that a baby is able to pronounce is *uma*. A baby says *uma* for anything and everything. Since food is the most important thing to babies, food comes to monopolize this sound. This infantile habit continues into adulthood, so delicious things are later described as *umai*. His conclusion was that worries about life's problems are all traceable to *uma-uma*, the food problem. Sounds more like a storyteller's anecdote, does it not?"

"Utter nonsense."

"Yes. But interviewing is mostly nonsense."

"And is it not discourteous to speak such nonsense to you?"

"No, I do not mind it so much. They are mostly fools. On the other hand, there are times I meet someone who is very earnest but holds extravagant ideas. The other day I had to listen to an extravagant theory of romantic love."

"Nakano, I presume."

"You know him? He talked with great enthusiasm."

"He was one of my classmates."

"Oh, I see. He calls himself Nakano Shuntai, if I remember correctly. He must be a man of leisure, to take such views seriously."

"He is a rich man."

"That accounts for the fact the he lives in a magnificent house. Are you his intimate friend?"

"Yes, we used to be very intimate. But I regret that our friendship is no longer what it was, because he now has a sweetheart or fiancée, and he has neglected me of late."

"In that case you need not associate with him. You will lose nothing. Ha, ha, ha!"

"But I cannot help feeling like a solitary being in the world, and I dislike feelings of loneliness."

"To be solitary in the world is all right," said Dōya-sensei, using the same phrase from a moment ago.

Takayanagi wanted to say, "That may be all right for you," as he had said before, but no longer had the courage.

"Since ancient times, the man intent on an enterprise has been a solitary being. If you rely on a friend, you cannot hope to accomplish anything. You may become isolated from your own relatives. You may be taunted by your own wife or jeered at by your maid."

"If I should find myself in such circumstances, I should be unable to survive the bitterness."

"In that case you will never become a man of letters."

Takayanagi looked down in silence.

"When I was your age, I did not suspect that the world was so bad as this. But such is the actual condition of our world. Don't think I am exaggerating. Jesus, Confucius, and other sages suffered for their causes, but when we writers praise their suffering while living a life of comfort, then we are counterfeit men of letters. We have no right to praise those great men."

Though he was in great distress now, Takayanagi clung to a slender thread of hope that the time would arrive soon when he could emerge a new man. But his slender thread of hope was half-broken by Dōya's warning, and there was little promise of rising from the present slough of despond.

"Takayanagi-san!"

"Yes."

"This is a hard world to live in, I tell you."

"Yes, so it is."

"You realize it, don't you?" said Dōya, smiling sadly.

"Yes, I realize it clearly enough, but is my life going to be so painful indefinitely? . . ."

"You cannot endure it? Your parents are still alive?"

"Only my mother, who lives in the country."

"A mother only?"

"Yes."

"Well, you are fortunate to have one parent, if not both."

"I am not fortunate. She is quite old. I ought to do something for her comfort. Upon graduating, I had hoped to be able to do something for her, but . . ."

"I see. There are more and more graduates nowadays, so that it is getting difficult to find a job. Have you ever considered taking a teaching job in the country?"

"I think about it from time to time."

"And then you give up on the idea. It is true that there is little opportunity for promotion. I have quite a bit of experience myself as a country school teacher."

"Sensei, you were . . .," said Takayanagi, but proceeded further, too shy to speak of the event from his past.

"Yes?" asked Dōya innocently.

"You are editing *The World* magazine, I am told. Is that so?"

"Yes, I have recently assumed editorial duties at the magazine."

"This month's issue featured an article titled 'Emancipation and Attachment,' signed by a certain Yūseishi. Is the author . . . ?"

"Yes, it is I. Did you read it?"

"Yes, I read it with great interest. If I may say so, your essay expressed my sentiments from a much more elevated point of view. From reading it, I derived not only much benefit but also exquisite pleasure."

"I thank you. Then you are my sympathizer. Probably the only one in the whole world. Ha, ha, ha!"

"You do yourself an injustice in thinking so," said Takayanagi in a serious tone.

"Do you think so? Then I must congratulate myself all the more. But I have never known a single person to praise my writing. You are the sole exception."

"From now on, I shall praise everything from your pen."

"Ha, ha, ha, ha! If there were as many as one hundred same-thinking people, I should be most satisfied. —By the way, I do encounter some comical things from time to time. The other day I had a visit from a queer fellow."

"What was he?"

"He was a businessman. I don't know from where he heard about me, but he said, 'I hear you edit a magazine, so I assume you can write.'"

"Indeed!"

"I said I could write at any rate. Then the man asked me to write an advertisement for his eye medication."

"What an absurd request!"

"In return for my writing, he said he would place an advertisement in the magazine for his medicine, called Ten-mei-sui Clear Eye Drops."

"What a queer name! —Did you write the advertisement?"

"No, in the end I declined. And the story gets curiouser. The day the medicine went on sale, the chemist's shop was to send up a balloon."

"As a celebration?"

"No, to advertise the medicine. But as a balloon sails noiselessly in the sky, in order to be noticed by people, it is necessary to make them look up."

"Quite right."

"So the man asked me to make people look up at the sky."

"But how were you to do that?"

"Well, on that day, while I was walking along the street or riding the tram, I was to look up, notice the balloon, and cry out repeatedly, 'Look! A balloon! It must be an advertisement for Ten-mei-sui Clear Eye Drops!'"

"Ha, ha, ha! Well, I should say he was making a fool of you to request such a thing."

"A request as amusing as it was foolish. I said to him, 'You need not call on me for such a simple task. Why not hire a ricksha man?' And he said, 'No, a ricksha man will not inspire trust. We need a serious-looking, mustachioed gentlemen or people will see through our trick."

"How impudent! What kind of man was he?"

"What kind of man? Well, just an ordinary man. He came to hire a man for deceiving the public. A rather simple fellow! Ha, ha, ha!"

"I am really surprised. I would have thrashed him."

"If you were to thrash every such man, there would be no end to it. You are angry, but you must remember that our present society is mostly composed of men like that."

Takayanagi did not quite agree with that generalization. The shadow of the drying socks cast on the shoji doors had disappeared. Through the half-opened door, he could see a shoe-brush, its edges muddy. In a corner of the tiny garden bloomed a single chrysanthemum, reflecting Sensei's honest poverty. Indifferent to nature as Takayanagi was, this flower alone he thought beautiful. Just beyond the cedar hedge he saw a large persimmon tree with red, half-ripened fruit, like coral against the azure sky. The noise of a bird-clapper sent the crows flying.

"Your home is very quiet."

"Yes. The noise you heard was the priest of Takodera scaring away birds. He has nothing to do but drive away crows all day. His is an enviable quiet life."

"The persimmon tree is full of ripe fruit."

"But they are astringent. I wonder why the priest jealously guards those worthless, puckery persimmons. —I noticed you have a strange cough at times. Are you healthy? You look quite thin. It will never do to be so lean. One's body is one's capital, you know."

"You are lean, too, are you not?"

"I? Indeed, I am lean. Lean, but healthy."

7

White butterflies on white flowers;
Little butterflies on little flowers—
Confusing they are to the eye,
Flying about the flowers.

Long sorrows in long hair!
Dark sorrows in dark hair—
The sorrows nestling there
Make the hair entangled!

The late autumn's blast, blowing but idly;
Do we idly exist in this sorrowful world?
White butterflies confusing to the eye,
Dark hair hopelessly entangled.

The woman finished singing the song. The man listened to her voice, imagining that a gem stirred in a silver bowl by a delicate snow-white finger would produce a sound like her voice.

"You have sung excellently. With a little more practice to increase your volume, you will be able to sing splendidly in a large hall. Would you not like to test your voice at the next concert?"

"Test my voice? No!"

"Well then, perform as a professional?"

"I am not yet a professional singer."

"Then you will not sing at all?"

"How could I sing before all those people? I would be too shy to open my mouth."

"How do you like the poem in the new style?"

"I like it very much."

"May I take a picture of you standing and singing?"

"A photograph?"

"You dislike having your photograph taken?"

"It's not that I dislike having my photograph taken, but that you will show it to people."

"If you dislike having it shown to others, then I alone shall admire it."

The woman said nothing and looked aside. In her collar, patterned with scattered plum blossoms, she wore a pin, whose brilliance could be mistaken for Venus, which attracted the man's eye. In the direction of her gaze stood a three-foot-high shelf, on the lower half of which was placed a rectangular Cochin chinaware pot containing an orchid, its slender leaves ready to quiver at the touch of incense smoke. On the top shelf stood a replica of the Venus de Milo, looking dream-like in the shadowy darkness of the corner of the room. The woman's eye fell on the nude statue at once.

"That statue?" she asked.

"A copy, of course. The original is in the Louvre in Paris. But even the copy is splendid. The torsion of the upper part of the body and the direction of her legs are perfectly balanced. If the statue were complete, it would be simply superb. But unfortunately, the arms are missing."

"The original too has no arms?"

"Yes, as the original is without arms, so is the copy."

"And its subject?"

"Venus, the goddess of love," said the man stressing the word "love."

"Venus!" The Venus was being scrutinized by long-lashed eyes meant to dissolve it. Under her rapt gaze, the plaster statue seemed to warm, and its round breasts seemed to rise and fall with her breathing. The woman herself was a shining Venus.

"I see," she said, under her breath.

"If you look on her so intently, she will begin to move."

"So this is the goddess of love?" she said, turning her face to full view at last.

"It is you who are the goddess of love," he was going to say, but when his eyes met hers, he hesitated. Speaking the words would have altered her facial expression. To destroy the look of wonder, appeal, and trust in her eyes at this instant would be a crime as great as breaking the arms of Venus.

"To my mind she looks too noble . . .," she said, irritated by the man's failure to answer her question. She inclined her head, at the same time changing her expression of her own accord. He sorely regretted it.

"Yes, a little too severe. It is not sufficiently expressive of love."

"It impresses me as being somewhat cold."

"Yes, you are right. The word 'cold' hits the mark. I also have thought there was something strange about her features, but I could not put my finger on it. Cold. That's it. Cold is the very word for it."

"Why do you suppose the sculptor made the goddess of love like this?"

"Well, as he belonged to the school of Pheidias, he must have adopted this severe style."

"Do you like the cast of her features?"

Comparing the statue with herself, the woman sought to uncover her lover's tastes. She felt uneasy, thinking if he loved Venus, he could not love her. She forgot that Venus was a goddess.

"Do I like it? Is it not fine? It is a masterpiece of the ancient and modern world!"

The woman's appreciation was instinctive; the man's was partly traditional. Influenced by lectures on aesthetics he only halfway understood, he had no courage to assent to the woman's opinion. He did not realize that learning could be self-deceptive. While being deceived by learning himself, he thought the woman's unprejudiced judgment wrong.

"It is a masterpiece of ancient and modern art!" he repeated, partly to educate his sweetheart's sense of taste.

"Oh?" was all she said. Her unbiased impression received the first moment could not be wiped out by a single remark of a learned man.

"As a matter of fact, I have some unpleasant associations with Venus."

"What kind of associations?" she asked gently, placing one hand over the other. About two inches above her wrists were exposed, while the rest of her arms were hidden in the soft sleeves. Her kimono was of pink silk with a design of silver rain in intervals of heavy lines and light lines.

It was pleasant to see the fine fingers of the hand on top, each of which tapered off in a rounded shape to a gleaming nail. To be fine, fingers must be long and slender and yet provided with flesh soft enough to keep their delicate shape. Each finger must differ slightly from another, yet there must be harmony between them as a whole. There are fewer people with beautiful fingers than people with beautiful faces. A person with beautiful fingers must be in want of a precious ornament.

On a long slender finger the woman wore a brilliant object.

"I have never seen that ring before."

"This?" She separated her hands, placed one over the other, and played with the shiny object on her right hand. "Father bought it for me the other day."

"Is it a diamond?"

"I believe so. It was bought at Tenshōdō, the jewelers."

"You should not importune your father too much."

"Not at all. On the contrary, it was Father who decided to buy it for me."

"Well, what an extraordinary phenomenon."

She laughed and said, "Indeed, it was! But do you know the story?"

"How should I know? I am not a detective."

"That's why I ask if you know the reason."

"That's why I said I don't know."

"Shall I tell you?"

"Yes, please do."

"I will tell you, but you must not laugh. You know there were horse

57

races at Ikegami the other day. Father went there, and—"

"And what did he do? He found it on the ground?"

"What an unpleasant thing to say. You're insulting."

"But you say nothing more and keep me in suspense."

"Then I shall proceed. He placed a bet."

"You surprise me. Your father bets on the horses?"

"No, usually he does not, but on that occasion he did, on a whim."

"Then he does bet on the horses."

"Yes, he placed a bet. And he won five hundred yen."

"I see. And he bought the ring with his winnings."

"Well, yes."

"May I see it?" he asked, touching the brilliant stone.

A ring is a magical thing. Shakespeare wrote several eventful scenes based on a ring. The invisible tie that binds together a young man and woman is love, and what makes love tangible is a ring. The gemstone sat immovably and peacefully where a threefold band of gold looped together. In all its brilliance, it could not be removed without breaking the gold waves in which it was set, akin to the intertwined fate of the lovers, neither of whom could live without the other. The man gazed at the white finger and the ring upon it.

"It might have been a ring like this," said the man. The woman sat down on a sofa next to him.

"In olden times, a certain art collector excavated a bronze statue of Venus and placed it in his garden under a fragrant Chinese almond tree."

"Is this a story? You began so abruptly."

"One day he was playing tennis. . . . "

"Wait a minute. I do not follow you. Who was playing tennis? The man who excavated the statue?"

"It was a laborer who excavated the statue. But it was the man's master who had it dug up who was playing tennis."

"It does not matter either way."

"No, you should not confuse the master and the man."

"But it was the man who dug out the statue who was playing tennis?"

"If you insist, then so be it: the man who dug out the statue was playing tennis."

"I am not insistent. Then it was the man who had the statue dug out who was playing tennis. Does that satisfy you?"

"It does not matter either way."

"My! Are you angry? Do you not see I have just said by way of apology that it was the man who had the statue dug up who was playing tennis?"

"Ha, ha, ha! You need not apologize. To come back to the story, while the man was playing tennis, he found his ring got in the way and prevented him from wielding his racket properly. So he took it off and considered where he should put it so he would not lose sight of it since it was so small. This was an important ring, a wedding ring."

"Who was he to marry?"

"Who? Well, that's a bit difficult. He was going to marry a certain young lady."

"Oh, why don't you tell the story, and stop holding back her name!"

"I'm not holding back anything."

"Then please tell the story, won't you? Who was the other party?"

"I am at a loss. I have forgotten her name."

"Now I see you have been equivocating."

"But I have lent out my copy of Mérimée's book, so I cannot look for the name."

"So you have lent the book to someone. Very well!"

"How disturbing. I cannot proceed now, because I have forgotten her name. I must give up the story for today. But by next time I shall have ascertained the lady's name and shall tell you the story over again."

"Oh, you! How can you leave off right when I was getting interested?"

"But I do not know the name."

"Then proceed to the next part."

"Then you do not mind her not having a name?"

"No."

"In that case, I might have proceeded with the story sooner. After considering for some time where to put the ring, he came up with an idea: to place the ring on the little finger of Venus."

"What a clever idea. And poetic, too."

"When the tennis match was over, he forgot all about the ring. He did not remember until he had already gone out to the country to fetch the young lady. Unable to recover the ring, he decided instead to buy her another one that was good enough, and he gave it as an engagement ring to his bride to be."

"What a disgusting man. How heartless he was."

"But he could not do otherwise, having forgotten the original ring at home.

"He had forgotten because he was heartless."

"As for me, I should never have forgotten. But as he was a foreigner, he forgot."

"You call him a foreigner!?" she said with a little laugh.

"After all, the betrothal went off satisfactorily, and he came home with his fiancée. On their wedding night . . . " here he paused intentionally.

"What happened on their wedding night?"

"On their wedding night the Venus in the garden came into the entrance hall with heavy footfalls."

"Oh! How uncanny!"

"With heavy footfalls she came up the stairs."

"How terrible!"

"She opened the door to the bedroom."

"How gruesome."

"If you find it gruesome, I shall break off the story."

"But how does the story end?"

"Well, with heavy footfalls she arrived at the door of the bedroom."

"Please skip that part and just tell me what happened in the end."

"Then I will skip the intervening part. On the morrow the man was found cold and dead. Parts of his body that had come under Venus's touch had turned purple. Or so they say."

"Oh! How uncanny!" she said, knitting her brows.

When a beautiful woman knits her brows, it is like a rich dish spiced with vinegar. A man drunk on the sweetness of love sometimes finds it delicious.

Under dark, crescent-shaped eyebrows, drawn closer together, her bright eyes were expressive of sympathy. The man was absorbed in watching her features.

"What about his wife?" she asked, anxious about the fate of the person of her own sex.

"She fell ill and was taken to the hospital."

"Did she recover?"

"Well, that is all I remember. I wonder what became of her."

"Why should she not recover? She committed no offense."

Her lower lip, sumptuous but not thick, trembled. The man did not think her silly, but warm-hearted. Theirs was a world of love. Love is a most serious sport. But since it is a sport, it always disappears when lovers face a crisis. Fortunate are those who can afford to play the sport of love.

Love is serious, and being serious, love is deep. At the same time, love is a sport; and being a sport, love is buoyant. What is at once deep yet buoyant is seaweed on the ocean floor and love between the young.

"Ha, ha, ha! You need not worry. The wife gets better, I can assure you," the man guaranteed her without consulting his Mérimée.

Love is an illusion; love is also enlightenment. Love absorbs into itself all things in the universe and endows them with a preternatural life in a moment. Hence, love is an illusion. Seen through the eyes of love, the three thousand worlds are golden. The cosmos reflected in the heart of love is a cosmos of infinite love. Hence, love is enlightenment. But a person who breathes the air of love does not know illusion from enlightenment. He merely attracts and is attracted by others. Nature abhors a vacuum; love

60

abhors isolation.

"I feel truly sorry for her. Suppose I should ever find myself in her situation, what should I do?"

A lover has exceedingly deep sympathy for himself. Only when he is satisfied with the joys of love, can he transcend himself and sympathize with others, because of these deep feelings of sympathy. When he is disappointed in love, he can transcend himself and pity others more than usual, because of these deep feelings. Successful in love, a man considers himself benevolent; unsuccessful in love, a man still considers himself benevolent. Whether successful or not, love runs a straight course and judges all things by the standard of love. Successful love is a horse drawing a carriage with sympathy riding in it; unsuccessful love is a horse drawing a carriage with self-pity riding in it. Love is a most self-centered thing.

Two most self-centered and benevolent lovers were performing the serious and deep sport of love in a beautifully decorated room. The world outside the room was the desolate season of autumn. The world of autumn was making people like Dōya-sensei suffer, and causing people like Takayanagi to feel lonely. But our two lovers were benevolent people through and through.

"You were with Takayanagi-san at the concert the other day, I recall."

"We had no appointment to attend, but as I happened to meet him on the way, I invited him to come with me. I found him standing alone in front of the zoo and looking down sadly at fallen cherry leaves. I felt sorry for him, so I brought him with me.

"You did well to bring him. He's not ill, is he?"

"He was coughing a bit. But I don't think it is anything serious."

"But he was looking very unwell."

"He is so nervous that he will often worry himself sick. But when I try to console him he becomes sarcastic. He seems to be getting stranger and stranger."

"I am sorry for him. I wonder what's wrong?"

"What's wrong with him is that he chose to be solitary, and he regards all the world as his enemy. I don't know what to do with him."

"Was his heart broken?"

"I have never heard anything of the kind. Perhaps he needs a wife to look after him."

"Yes, someone to look after him."

"But looking after someone who is so hard to please—that's asking too much. He would make his wife miserable."

"But I think that if he had a wife his condition would improve."

"That might help him improve to some extent, but he is constituted that way. He tends to look on the dark side of things. He has contracted the illness of pessimism."

At this she laughed a little laugh and said, "How did he develop such a disease?"

"I don't know. It may be hereditary or the result of some experience in his early childhood."

"Have you heard of anything of that nature?"

"No, I have not. I am not one to inquire into such things. And besides, he is not the sort of man to open up to others. If he were frank and unreserved, I could comfort him in some way."

"Is he in dire straits?"

"If you mean strapped for cash, yes, he is in dire straits. But if I should offer him money for no reason, I should be in danger of being beaten by him."

"Considering he is a university graduate, he ought to be able to earn money enough."

"Of course he will. It is only a matter of time. But, impatient fellow that he is, he feels that immediately upon graduating he ought to have turned into an established writer, become famous, and live in comfort. But that is an impossible idea."

"Where was he born?"

"In Niigata Prefecture."

"That is a far away place. Niigata is a rice-producing prefecture. Was he born in a farming family?"

"Yes, he may be the son of a farmer. The mention of Niigata reminds me of something. Do you remember seeing a man who was just leaving as you arrived here last time?"

"Yes. The man with the long face and a moustache? What is he? I was surprised to see his wooden clogs. They were worn very thin, almost as thin as a pair of slippers."

"And yet he is quite self-complacent. Moreover, he is not an amiable man. However I tried to strike up a conversation, he was unresponsive."

"On what business did he come?"

"He came to interview me in his capacity as editor of *The World* magazine."

"To interview you? And did you give him your opinion?"

"Yes, I did. I have since received a copy of the magazine, so I shall show it to you later. I have reason to speak to you about that man, for there is a strange story about him. Takayanagi, while still in middle school in his native prefecture, was taught by him. Takayanagi is a Bachelor of Literature, as you know, but that man is also a literary person."

"Oh, is he? I am surprised."

"It so happened that Takayanagi and other students played many mischievous tricks on him, eventually driving him away from school."

"They banished him? What a cruel thing to do?"

"Now that Takayanagi finds himself in dire straits, he regrets what he did to his teacher, imagining how he must have suffered over the loss of his job. He says he will apologize to his former teacher, if he ever sees him again."

"And as a result of losing his job he has been reduced to such bitter circumstances? I really sympathize."

"Well. As you see, I learned that the man is now editor of *The World* magazine. So I told the news to Takayanagi on our way back from the concert."

"Do you think Takayanagi has been to see him already?"

"He may have been."

"For driving his teacher away like that, he ought to apologize as soon as possible."

Here the conversation on the subject between the benevolent young people came to an end.

"What do you say to going into the other room and enjoying ourselves with the company?"

"But aren't you going to take a picture?"

"I completely forgot. Please let me take your picture, by all means. I can take rather artistic pictures, you know. Those taken by professional photographers are usually in bad taste. Photography has made great strides over the past five or six years, so that now it is a respectable art. As for ordinary pictures, they are on the whole the same, whoever the photographer may be. But today's photographs are quite different in tone, according to the individual tastes of the photographer. Nowadays they make use of various devices. They may omit the irrelevant, soften the tone of the whole, or express the play of strong light on the whole. Already specialists have appeared, some in natural scenery, others in portraiture."

"Are you a specialist in portraiture, then?"

"I? Well, I will become a specialist in portraiture of you."

"Oh, you are incorrigible!"

The diamond in the ring sparkled, and a delicate arm inside a rustling pink sleeve slid down toward the man's knee, her fingertips lightly brushing against him.

The conversation of the benevolent couple ended in taking photographs.

8

Autumn gradually deepened. The sound of insects diminished. Dōya-sensei, absorbed in writing his life-work, and with no time to spare for other matters, did not notice the growing cold of the passing autumn or the weakening sound of insects, or the unkind attitude of people toward him, or the dirt under his fingernails, or that all the persimmons had fallen from the tree at Takodera. The mission of Dōya-sensei was to move society by his own efforts in a direction that it ought to be moved. His calling was to move society, even if only a step, toward the lofty, the great, the just. He cared about nothing else.

Takayanagi was a different matter. Unlike Dōya-sensei, who noticed nothing, Takayanagi noticed everything. He noticed people in the street looking askance at him, the piercing autumn wind, the number of wild geese flying across the sky and their indistinct cries, the beauty of women, the value of money. He noticed the transience of his own life, treated as he was by the world as if he were so much dust in the wind. Come evening, he gnawed at the bone of suffering of this floating world and knew his boarding-house dinner would consist of nothing more than a potato. Too well he knew his own natural inclinations, and his sickness was to magnify them out of proportion. Of all the innumerable people of the world, there was not one to cure him of this sickness. With no one to cure him of his sickness, all the innumerable people of the world were as good as nonexistent to him. He lived a solitary life, not solitary in the sense that he was complacent enough to forego the company of others, but drearily solitary while hungering for sympathy and thirsting for company. Nakano called him morbid, and he thought so himself. But it was the world that made him morbidly solitary, and now the world looked on his critical illness with indifference. Not satisfied with only having made him ill, the world had to snuff out what little life remained. Takayanagi could not but curse the world.

In Dōya-sensei's view the world was a place to work for the sake of others; in Takayanagi's view the world was a place to work for his own sake. In a world where he lived for others, Dōya felt no regret that no one offered a helping hand. In a world where he lived for himself, Takayanagi felt the world that cared nothing for him was cruel.

Such is the difference between one who exists for others and one who exists for himself. Such is the difference between one who leads others and one who relies on others. Such is the difference, even when both are solitary individuals. Takayanagi was not aware of these differences.

From his grimy, chilly futon, resting his head on a pillow, and in need of a haircut, Takayanagi looked out at the phoenix tree in the small garden. Whenever his eyes grew tired from writing, he always looked out at this phoenix tree. Whenever he felt wretched from translating *How to Teach Geography*, he always looked out at this phoenix tree. Even when he was at a loss for the right expression in writing a letter, he looked out at this phoenix tree. As well he might, for in the small neglected garden, three *tsubo* in size, there was nothing else to look at.

Especially as he had been feeling ill of late and in no mood for work, he gazed at the tree from dawn to dusk, with his cheek resting drowsily on his cheap desk.

The first leaf to fall, as the saying goes, is a harbinger of things to come, but, in truth, sad autumn always assails the phoenix tree first. When people begin to put on lined kimonos, they hardly notice the rustle of leaves falling on the hedge. Yet the next morning more leaves will rustle to the ground. As people close the rain shutters against the chill, still another leaf rustles to the ground. The leaves at last turn yellow.

From the backside of green leaves now gradually decaying, a resin color rises up in a thin flow, growing darker and darker with each passing night of cold, on the verge of their rustling dance of death.

The wind blows. Coming from who knows where, it sweeps through the trees. One or two leaves begin to fall from the yellowed treetop, scarcely seen to shake, but all the rest are untouched.

With the frost of each night the resin darkens until black veins streak the brown leaves. Raking the fallen leaves produces a crackling sound, like crunching on a rice cookie. The black streaks spread over the entire leaf. The end is near.

A wind comes up, blowing through the garden hedge and from under the veranda. The leaves whose end is near then fall in thick succession. Even those whose end is in question detach themselves from treetops. Against the moonlit sky one can count the number of bare, bony branches.

Insects eat the few remaining leaves. A single hole appears in a dark brown leaf, and another in its neighbor, and another, and another, until the leaves are riddled with holes. A forlorn feeling sweeps over the leaves, and people looking at them say to themselves, "How forlorn!" And a wind comes up and scatters them all away.

When Takayanagi happened to look up, this complete process had transformed the phoenix tree, leaving it bare. On the end of a branch stretching toward the window, a single, hole-riddled leaf still clung.

"How lonely!" Takayanagi whispered to himself.

Since last month he had developed a strange cough, and at first he had paid no attention to it. Recently, his coughing was less wrenching and more hollow sounding. And it wasn't just the coughing, but he sometimes felt feverish. Just when he sensed a fit of coughing coming on, it would stop. And just when it stopped and he thought he could get some work done, it started up again. Takayanagi bent his neck to one side.

He thought about seeing a doctor, but resolving to see a doctor would be admitting to himself that he was a sick man. Admitting to himself that he was a sick man would be like confessing his own guilt. Until one is judged guilty of a crime, it is human nature to defend oneself against the charges. Takayanagi now defended his physical condition before having it diagnosed by a doctor. His defense was that his illness was a case of nerves. He was ignorant of that fact that neurosis is the twin brother of his actual disease.

He sometimes had night sweats, occasionally waking up with sweat in his eyes. He would awake in pitch dark and wish the darkness would last forever. Awakening to dawn and to the sound of voices and to the existence of the world was painful to him.

He closed his eyes against the dark to make it darker still, and he hid his head under the covers, never wanting to stick it out again. He slept hoping that he would be transported to the other world while still asleep. But a new day would dawn and sunlight would shine mercilessly through the window.

Several times a day he took out his watch and checked his pulse. Each time his pulse was not normal, beating too rapidly or beating irregularly, but never beating predictably. Each time he coughed up phlegm, he would scrutinize it with large eyes. He was comforted that at least there was no trace of blood.

Finding comfort that his phlegm was not mixed with blood, he would have to find his next comfort in being alive when his phlegm is mixed with blood. Takayanagi, perhaps doomed to find comfort in still being alive, was not a man satisfied to be merely alive. People often experience this paradoxical situation. They desire a happy life and cannot disavow the necessity of enjoying a happy life. Whereas mere existence may not be the goal, they must sustain all manner of suffering because life is a prerequisite to happiness. Those who live with this paradox, adrift in the world of dust and struggling against death, are conscious that each day carries them closer to the grave. Like debtors who borrow more money to pay off their debts, their condition does not improve. Nothing could be more wretched.

Takayanagi crawled out of bed. Putting on a black cotton coat over his padded kimono of polished material in a splashed pattern, he sat down at his desk to do some translation work. Unused during the past four or five days, his desk was covered with a fine layer of dust blown in through a tear in the shoji doors. His ink-stone looked white. Not even bothering to blow away the dust, Takayanagi poured water into the ink-stone. He did not use

66

a water-holder, however, but filled the ink-stone from a small glass bottle containing chrysanthemums, which he held to one side while pouring. Rubbing the wrong end of the Kōbai-en ink-stick produced a grating sound. Takayanagi knit his brows. Takayangi was one who bit his lip when something unpleasant occurred, instead of taking precautions to prevent the unpleasant from happening. He was too sensitive to endure unpleasant things, but too reckless to take preventative measures.

Placing some manuscript paper on his desk, he wrote feverishly for an hour, producing two or three pages, and finally put down his brush. Outside the window the lonely leaf on the phoenix tree still remained.

"How lonely!" Takayanagi repeated under his breath.

While he looked on, the leaf moved slightly up and down. He expected it to fall at any moment, but the wind stopped.

Takayanagi took out a roll of paper and began to write a letter to his mother in his hometown.

How are you getting along in this season when the air grows colder day by day? I hope you are keeping well. I am fine. After writing thus far, he thought for a while, and then he tore off what he had written and put the paper in his mouth. He chewed it up and spat it out into the garden.

The solitary leaf moved again, swaying back and forth a few times. No sooner had it ceased to sway when a gust of wind came up and dropped the decayed leaf to the ground.

"It's fallen. It's fallen," Takayanagi cried, as if it were an important event.

Soon after, he opened a three-foot-wide wardrobe and took out a brown trilby. Going out the gate, he looked up at the sky. The passing autumn's heavy pall of clouds hung over him.

"Obaasan! Obaasan!" he called to the landlady.

"Coming," she said, putting down her dust cloth and going out to him.

"Please bring my umbrella. It's on the veranda of my room."

He was set on going for a walk even if it rained. With no destination in mind, he intended just to walk. A tram runs with no idea why it runs. Takayanagi was conscious of walking, but like the tram car, was unconscious as to why. Cruelty made him walk without business in mind, without a goal, even without a desire to walk. Since cruelty made him walk, he had no enemy; if he wanted an enemy, he had to face the originator of the cruelty. The originator of the cruelty was society. Takayanagi walked alone in an inimical world. No matter how long he walked, he was as lonely as ever.

Drops of rain began to fall at intervals. This must be what is known as the first shower of autumn. Under the eaves of a tofu shop, the dregs of tofu making were mounded in a wooden tub. The peak of the mountain of dregs was flattened, and steam issuing from all sides was carried into the street by the wind. At a salt-curing shop, a filleted salmon showed its dull-red flesh. Next to it dried whitebait curled whitely. At a dried-bonito shop, a boy painstakingly polished dried bonito from Tosa with a brush, buffing it to a fine gloss. The back of the shop was enlivened by a bright-green artificial pine for use in decorating wedding gifts of dried bonito. At a tea shop, an apprentice slowly ground green tea leaves in a stone mortar. Beside him a clerk sipped tea while looking out on the street.

"Hey! Watch out!" somebody cried, pushing Takayanagi aside.

A ricksha sped by carrying a grand-looking gentleman in a black formal overcoat bearing his family crest, and wearing a bowler. The passenger was high-spirited. The person on foot, brushed aside, was out of luck. He had to take the words "Hey! Watch out!" on the chin. Takayanagi walked on like a ghost.

He passed through a bronze torii. On the stone pavement leading to the shrine, five or six pigeons walked about in the rain. Watching them, a young dancing-girl held up an open paper umbrella with a brown bulls-eye design. Her hair was done up in the Chinese style, and she wore a long overcoat on her back and a pair of rain clogs on her naked feet. Two students looked down from an upstairs window of a boarding house and evaluated her charms. A geisha worshipping at the shrine clapped her hands, rang the bells, and threw some coins into the coffer. Passing Takayanagi in her black crepe coat with a family crest of three oak leaves, the geisha gave him a co-quettish glance. Takayanagi felt a lead weight tug at his heart.

He descended thirty-six stone steps and came to a street on which trams ran noisily back and forth. The wall of the Iwasaki mansion grimly dominated the block. Takayanagi thought how he would like to dash his head against the wall in an attempt to destroy it. The shower had since ceased, and five or six people were queued up at the tram stop. A tall man in a black family-crested coat and holding a furled European umbrella stood and looked at the sky.

"Sensei!" the solitary Takayanagi cried out.

"Well, fancy meeting you here, of all places. Out for a walk, I see."

"Yes," replied Takayanagi.

"I admire your taking a walk in spite of the weather. Three times around the wall of Iwasaki mansion makes for good exercise. Ha, ha, ha!"

"You are out for a walk too, Sensei?"

"No. I have little time to spare for a walk. I am always busy. I had to go the Ueno Library to do a bit of research."

Meeting Dōya-sensei this way lifted Takayanagi's spirit. He felt some-what buoyed by fact that there was someone in the present world who could be complacent in the face of solitude.

"Sensei, won't you take a little walk?"

"I don't mind walking a little. But in which direction? Not toward Ueno, because I have just come from there."

"Any direction is fine with me."

"Then let us go up this slope to Hongo Street. I go home that way."

The two set out along the tramline. Takayanagi felt that his customary solitude had suddenly turned into companionship. The sky seemed more vast than before. He even thought that a ricksha puller wouldn't dare to push him aside.

"Sensei?"

"What is it?"

"I little while ago I was pushed aside by a ricksha man."

"A close call, was it? Were you hurt?"

"No, I was not hurt, but I was angry."

"I see. But it is no use getting angry. Anger may be useful, however, depending on what one does with it. In olden times Watanabe Kazan experienced the calamity of accidentally running into the vanguard of Lord Matsudaira's retinue. Writing about the event, Kazan referred to it as 'The Honorable Outrage of Lord Matsudaira's Procession.' Don't you think his phrase clever? Behind the respectful 'honorable' lies a fine spirit of resistance—his high spirit. Go home and write in your diary of the 'Honorable Outrage of the Ricksha Man.'"

"Who was Lord Matsudaira?"

"Nothing is known about him now. Had he been worthy of being known to posterity, he would not have allowed such outrage in his retainers. Kazan's inspiration is remembered to this day, but nobody knows anything about Lord Matsudaira!"

"It is pleasant to view the matter in that way. But when I see the walls of Iwasaki mansion, I want to demolish them by smashing my head against them."

"If it were possible to demolish them by striking your head against them, others might have done so before you. Banish those silly ideas and produce a resounding literary work instead. Then your fame will outlive the Iwasaki's, I can assure you."

"But I am not allowed to produce any literary works."

"Who prevents you?"

"It is not people who prevent me. But my personal circumstances."

"Are you ill?" asked Dōya-sensei, looking closely at Takayanagi's face from the side. His pale cheeks were faintly aglow with fever. Dōya inclined his head to one side.

"I noticed when climbing the slope you were short of breath. Is something the matter with you?"

When others hit upon something about yourself that you were

attempting to hide even from yourself, you cannot help feeling disappointed, finally seeing the thing clearly. Dōya's words had hit the mark and plunged Takayanagi into a dark pit. There are not a few people who sympathize with others in this consciously cruel way.

"Sensei!" Takayanagi stopped in the street.

"Yes?"

"Do I look like a sick man?"

"Well, yes. You look a bit pale."

"I might be consumptive after all?"

"Consumptive? I wouldn't think so."

"I want you to speak frankly."

"Have you ever suffered from tuberculosis?"

"It is hereditary. My father died of it."

"Oh, I see." Dōya paused, lost for an answer.

If you prick a tiny hole in a pig's bladder tightly filled with water, the pinprick will soon grow to the size of a coin. Once the subject was broached, Takayanagi could not stop, and could not wait for Dōya's response.

"Sensei, would you mind listening to my life story?"

"Not at all."

"My father was an official at the local post office. When I was six years old he was taken into police custody."

Not saying a word, Dōya walked leisurely with the narrator.

"Later I learned that he had embezzled public funds. But at the time I knew nothing of the matter. When I asked Mother about Father's absence, she would assure me each time, 'He'll be home soon. He'll be home soon.' But he never came home. He died in prison of tuberculosis. That's what I learned many years afterwards. Mother disposed of the house in town and moved to a neighboring village."

Two ricksha approached briskly from the opposite direction, carrying ladies whose hair was done in a chignon, in the Western fashion. Dōya and Takayanagi had to get out of the way, so their conversation was interrupted.

"Sensei?"

"Yes?"

"Consumption, you see, runs in our family. I am doomed."

"Have you seen a doctor?"

"No, I have not. It does not matter either way."

"You must not be so desperate. Even consumption is not always fatal."

Takayanagi smiled a bitter smile. A slight shower began to fall. They passed the Buddhist temple known popularly as Karatachi-dera, on the gate of which was posted a white sheet of paper bearing the notice "Lecture on the *Hekigan Roku*, The Blue Cliff Record." Students were streaming out of the girls' school, wearing colors of red, purple, and maroon, and spilling into the street.

"Sensei, is crime hereditary too?" asked Takayanagi, threading his way through the throng of girls.

"It is impossible."

"It may be impossible, but I am the son of a criminal just the same. It grieves me so."

"Certainly it is a painful thought, but you must try to forget it."

From the police station ahead, two criminals in handcuffs were being escorted out of the building by a policeman. The rain wetted the criminals' hair.

"I try to forget, but no sooner does the thought leave my mind, than it steals back."

Raising his voice a little, Dōya said, "But does your life belong to the past or to the future? The flower of your life has yet to bloom."

"My flower will wither before it blooms."

"Before it withers you must get to work."

Takayanagi remained silent. Looking back on his past, he saw crime; looking forward to the future, he saw disease. At present, he was earning his daily bread by his pen.

Dōya-sensei put his lips close to Takayanagi's ear and said, "You may think that you that you are the only solitary person in the world, but I too am a solitary man. Solitariness, however, is noble."

Takayanagi did not comprehend his meaning.

"Do you understand me?" asked Dōya-sensei.

"Noble. But why?"

"If you do not understand, you cannot possibly endure a solitary life. Though you are convinced that you stand on a higher plane than most people, they do not recognize this fact, so you feel solitary. If the higher plane were recognizable by others, they would be on it too. The kind of moral character that is comprehensible to geisha and ricksha men alike by definition must be lowly. If you get irritated or angry when they look down on you, it only shows that you assume you and they stand on the same level. Suppose you are on the same footing with them—you can never hope to produce any works but such as correspond to the character of these people. It is precisely because you are not equal to them that you may be able to produce works that promote high moral character. If you cannot produce a literary creation that promotes high moral character, it goes without saying that you will be looked down upon by them."

"I do not care about geisha or ricksha men."

"They only serve as an example of what I mean. I may as well take graduates as an example. To assume that graduates of the same university are similar is to confuse the form of education with its substance. If graduates of the same university are of equal stature, they will all of them leave behind undying fame, or they will all disappear into oblivion. If one strives to leave behind a name for posterity, one must presume that most of one's fellow graduates are going to die unknown. And that presumption implies one's admission that there is a great difference between oneself and one's colleagues. If you admit such a difference between yourself and others, but worry because others fail to understand you, then you commit a glaring self-contradiction."

"Then you intend to leave your name to posterity?"

"No. That is not the case with me. My argument was made for your sake. For as I understand, your ambition is to leave your name to posterity by creating fine literary works."

"If I may ask, what is your ambition?"

"I have no use for fame. I work for the sake of society only to satisfy myself. Whether the results prove dishonorable or scandalous, or drive me mad, I cannot help it. I work this way because I cannot satisfy myself otherwise. Considering that I can only satisfy myself by working like this, I realized that this is the way I should follow. Man cannot but follow his own way. Since man is a moral animal, I think it is the noblest thing for him to follow the way. If a man pursues the way, even the gods will have to make way for him. Much less can the walls of the Iwasaki mansion obstruct his course. Ha, ha, ha!"

Standing there with his threadbare bowler pushed back on his head, and carrying a sateen umbrella, Dōya's long face, that of a petty official, emitted a halo of light. Takayanagi was awestruck.

Passersby moved left and right in the street. Shops along the street took in customers and sent them on their way. Trams packed to capacity ran east and west. Like the forgotten and wasted dogs of a house in mourning, the two men walked the streets, one looking like a bureaucrat recently dismissed from his post, and one like a young, depraved student. Who would not think so? Dōya might be content with such an observation, but Shūsaku would resent it. The two parted company at the Yonchome intersection.

9

The small world of the villa, warmed by the sun of an Indian summer, was converted to a garden party in celebration of a wedding.

Love detests narrow-mindedness and hates monopolization. The overflowing affection of the loving couple washed over all their friends and acquaintances. Abundant wealth allowed the presence of many guests. Those who do not attend dislike the beckoning wind fanned by peace and harmony; they rather belong to the flock of wild geese that migrate to cold, snowy skies.

Perfect love tends to bring perfection to everything it touches. The couple's love even perfected the weather prone to the frequent showers of early winter. The sun shone perfectly overhead. So bright was the sun, a fact that all were conscious of, that no one dared to look at it without shading his eyes with his hand. No one among the prosperous dislikes a day of sunshine. Guests arrived from all quarters of the city.

Choosing cedar for its verdure, two thick pillars were decorated and joined together to form an arch. But the green of the cedar would be too severe; one who enters the kingdom of love must not pass through a gate of such austerity. The green must be softened with a warmer color. The color of mandarin oranges was the warm hue chosen to offset the green. Indian summer's color is yellow. The jewel-like oranges interspersed among the evergreen boughs released a scented breeze from the Southern seas. It was a scent that steals from the land of Ki when tens of thousands of oranges are lit up by the morning sun as it suddenly appears above the horizon, shooting sunbeams from one hill to the next, and giving way to the purple dawn. Those who enter through the arch as a rule are not allowed to leave unless intoxicated.

The new bride and groom stood under the arch. All such couples are of course new. Newly wedded husband and wife must be beautiful. Standing under the arch, the newlyweds, fresh and beautiful, impart some of their happiness to each arriving guest and again to each departing friend, and yet have happiness remaining to see them both into white-haired old age.

The man wore a black coat over striped trousers and occasionally fluttered a snow-white handkerchief about his breast. The woman wore a family-crested kimono. Its skirt had a gorgeous pattern, and her upper body seemed to rise gracefully from among the forms and colors of the pattern. Venus is said to have sprung from the foam of the sea, and this woman seemed to have sprung from the pattern of her kimono skirt.

Sunshine fell across the nape of her neck, throwing her shapely throat into pale shadow. Viewed from the side, her profile came into view from the thinning shadow. Above her face, purplish black hair was gathered up, floating over her forehead. The end of a gold hairpin, ornamented with scarlet cloisonné in the Nouveau style, protruded from the purple.

Love abhors the adamantine, never resting until all that is solid melts into air. The light itself, glittering from her eyes, was liquified. All that came into her line of vision, emanating from the depth of the mysterious sacred mirrors of her eyes, could not stray from the boundaries of ecstasy. The arriving guests, greeted by those eyes, enter the grounds in a rapturous frame of mind.

"Is Takayanagi-san coming?" she said in a whisper.

"Eh?" the man asked, bringing his ear nearer her lips. In the inner garden a brass band struck up the tune of *Echigo jishi*, The Lion Dance of Echigo. A majority of the guests had already assembled. The bride and bridegroom turned to their duty of host and hostess.

"Oh, yes. I had forgotten," the man said.

"Since most of the guests have arrived, we must go in, don't you think?"

"Oh, yes. We had better go in. But I shall be sorry if Takayanagi comes."

"You will be sorry if he comes when you are not here, you mean?"

"Yes. If he comes but does not find me here, he will turn around at the gate and go."

"But why?"

"Why? Because he has never been to such a party before. He makes himself solitary by choice. I cannot rest assured until I see him enter at the arch."

"Is he sure to come?"

"Yes, I am sure he will come, because I went to request his company. Once he promises to come—even if he doesn't want to—he will surely come. I am certain of it."

"Then, he is reluctant to come?"

"Reluctant? No, he is not, but he is indecisive, after all."

"How queer!" she said with a little laugh.

He is indecisive because of his lack of self-confidence. His lack of self-confidence is due to his fear that the world despises him. Nakano thinks him merely indecisive. His wife thinks him merely queer. The couple is oblivious to their own tendency toward indecisiveness. People who enter the world of the couple may live a life free of indecision, however indecisive they may be by nature.

"If he is coming, we had better stay here for his sake."

"Yes, he will come, I can assure you. Father and the others are inside to attend to the rest of the guests."

Love is benevolent. A benevolent man does not hesitate to sacrifice his own convenience for the sake of others. Bride and bridegroom continued to wait under the arch for Takayanagi's arrival. He must make an appearance by all means.

Among the guests arriving in carriages and ricksha, Takayanagi came with cautious step as if encroaching on enemy ground. The garden party was a sea of joyous harmony, and under the swell of the newlyweds' smile all are unconsciously assimilated and find a balmy spring in the beginning of winter. The approaching year-end returned to spring for the garden party, which for Takayangi was enemy ground.

Any place where wealth and power, pride and self-satisfaction prevailed was for Takayanagi a hostile country. At a distance of ten feet he saw the young man and his wife standing under the arch, but he did not recognize his friend in the man. They, who had sacrificed their convenience for his sake, at first glance thought him unworthy of their waiting. A third part of friendship is taken up in the clothing of one's friend. The friend in Nakano's mind and the friend approaching him now differed greatly. Among all of today's guests, Takayanagi's clothing was the most miserable. Love is luxurious, it will not recognize the value of the existence of anything apart from the beautiful. Women in particular do not recognize this value.

Seeing Takayanagi coming, both the husband and wife thought, "What in the world—?" When Takayanagi met their gaze, he thought, "What in the world—?"

After thinking "What in the world—?" one cannot retreat. Takayanagi advanced with uncertain steps. The couple quickly concealed their initial surprise behind the light of their love.

"Oh! I am glad you have come. I was beginning to feel anxious because you were so late." This much was honest truth; his impression of surprise was suppressed.

"I wanted to come earlier, but some business prevented me." This was a fact, but his surprise he kept back. In the course of human interaction, the "What in the world—?" invariably remains undisclosed. When these moments accumulate, they finally lead to a ruptured friendship without the quarreling. Not only close friends but also close married couples become estranged from each other by degrees with such surprises.

"This is my wife," said Nakano, introducing her to Takayanagi. To introduce one's beautiful wife to a lonely man is not an act of kindness but a crime. The one bathed in the light of love was too choked on happiness to care.

The wife said nothing and bowed modestly. Takayanagi seemed dazed.

"This way, please. We will accompany you," Nakano said, leading the way. About twenty yards across the garden they ran into a man with salt and pepper hair.

"I say. What a fine garden you have. I did not realize it was so vast. Today is my first time to see it, even though I have been invited by your father several times. But I was always busy. And it's so well cared for—a truly splendid garden!" The man spoke incessantly, reluctant to move along. Soon several others joined the small group.

"Yes, very fine!"

"How many acres?"

"For years I have been looking for a place around here."

Diverse voices surrounded the newlyweds. Takayanagi stood aloof and dejected.

A woman with her sleeves tucked up with a narrow sash came running and seized the man in the five-family-crested coat of thick black silk.

"Come with me, sir."

"Come with you? I have already partaken of enough elsewhere."

"That's not fair! And after I've come running for you!"

"You have no delicacies to offer at your booth, I am sure."

"Oh, but we do! You! Just come why don't you?!" she begged, tugging him by the arm.

The man allowed himself to be dragged along, fearing for the state of his expensive formal overcoat. They ran into Takayanagi. In surprise the man looked back with an apologetic expression on his face, but upon observing Takayanagi's looks and clothes, his expression suddenly changed.

"Dear me!" he said in a condescending manner, standing and staring at Takayanagi.

"Come, come! Never mind, just come with me!" the woman said, looking askance at Takayanagi and dragging the man away.

Takayanagi began to walk about ploddingly. The young couple, surrounded by strangers, was inaccessible. A long tent was erected in the middle of the lawn. Peeping inside, he saw in the darkness a row of large flower pots of chrysanthemums. He marveled that there still were such beautiful chrysanthemums so late in the season. Hundreds of long white petals radiated from the center and curled at the ends in all possible directions. Petals on a yellow one all curled inward, forming a sphere, as if to protect some treasure at the center. There was a potted pine as well. Apples were piled in a crystal dish, contrasting pleasantly with the white fresh tablecloth. The apples glowed despite the darkness of the tent. Mandarin oranges were mounded in a large dish. A loud laugh burst on Takayanagi's ears. Turning around in surprise, he found two young men in silk hats, all smiles.

"Quite strange!" one said.

"Weird, really. Perfect rustics!" said the other.

Takayanagi looked intently at them. One wore a patterned waistcoat with a narrow opening in front, his right thumb inserted in his waistcoat pocket, and his elbow protruding. The other lightly supported himself on a thin walking stick, the tip of his right rubber-soled shoe touching the ground, and balanced his slender body on his left foot.

"Completely like waiters!" said the one on his left foot.

Takayanagi thought for a moment that they were speaking about him. Then the one in the patterned waistcoat spoke.

"Exactly! To attend a garden party in swallowtail coats! They ought to know that much even if they have never traveled abroad."

In the distance Takayanagi noticed two men in swallowtail coats talking together. "Birds of a feather," he thought to himself. He then realized they were the ones being laughed at. He could not grasp why swallowtail coats were improper for a garden party.

At the far end of the lawn was a dance stage with reed screens serving as walls. A short red and white curtain hung above the front of the stage, and a red carpet covered a long platform toward the rear of the stage. On the platform sat three women with samisen for accompaniment and two women singers. In the middle of the stage, a woman, with her face thickly powered and wearing the traditional black-lacquered headgear of court nobles—hers made of golden paper—took a pole in hand and then dropped it, opened a gorgeous fan and then folded it, raised her long red sleeves above her eyes and then lowered them, and assumed various other poses. A large sheet of paper bearing some brushed black characters announced the entertainment: *Asazuma-bune*, The Ferry Boat at Asazuma. Takayanagi thought, "So this is *Asazuma-bune*," watching from behind the audience, and making himself small.

Proceeding along the left side of the stage, he came to a granite bridge over a pond, beyond which rose an artificial hill and a grove of pine trees. Through the pines he caught a glimpse of something like a shop curtain waving, and he heard the high-pitched sound of women laughing. Crossing the bridge, he suddenly changed his mind and retraced his steps. The brass band played forcefully, vibrating the atmosphere of the entire garden.

He slowly returned to the tent, and this time refrained from looking inside, which was buzzing with activity. Going round to the entrance, he found people packed to the walls, and inside he heard the sound of plates clinking. He could not see the newlywed couple anywhere.

While he was watching the goings on, a cry of "hurrah!" was sent up from within, drowning out the brass band. Another "hurrah!" responded from the granite bridge, a lost child of a hurrah. Takayanagi entered the tent awkwardly, like a customer going into the wrong shop.

A man, threading his way through the crowd holding a plate aloft, approached Takayanagi.

"Please take this. There is much more food, but it is inaccessible because of the crowd." Takayanagi wondered if it was being offered to him, for the man's eyes were not on him. From behind a cool voice said, "Thank you." A young lady of seventeen or eighteen, wearing a family-crested kimono of pink crepe, took the plate.

A man at her side grabbed a chair from the corner and, placing it in front of her, said, "Here, place your food on this chair." Takayanagi moved a few yards to the left. Two men stood smoking tobacco by a post of the tent, one in a Western suit and one in Japanese clothes.

"Have you given up cigars?"

"Yes, they say they are bad for the brain. But once you are accustomed to cigars, you will find cigarettes unsatisfactory. Even the best cigarettes will not satisfy you."

"Just considering the price, a three-sen cigarette cannot compare to a thirty-sen cigar."

"What brand do you smoke?"

"Try one of these," said the man in the Western suit, offering one from an alligator cigarette case.

"Egyptian, I see. These must cost fifty or sixty yen per hundred."

"They taste fine considering their price."

"Well, perhaps I will take up these cigarettes. Even if I smoke twenty of these a day, it will only cost me about twenty yen."

Twenty yen, the amount that the gentleman intended to reduce to smoke, was the sum total of Takayangi's monthly income.

Takayanagi proceeded another four feet to the left. Three men were engaged in a conversation.

"The other day, Nozoe spoke of how he established a synthetic fertilizer company . . .," said a bald-headed man with a flat nose and gold-capped teeth.

"Yes, it was a successful enterprise. He did well by it," said another man with a dark square face, like the metal clasp of an old-fashioned tobacco pouch.

"And your name was among the list of supporters, was it not?" said the salt-and-pepper haired man who had robbed Takayanagi of the company of Nakano and his wife.

"So it was," the bald head resumed. "Nozoe asked me if I would hold some shares. I said I'd rather not this time. But he insisted. 'At least 500 shares,' he urged. 'As a matter of fact, I have already reserved them in your name.' What could I do? I let the matter be, and Nozoe immediately departed for Kyushu. A fortnight later, when I went to my office, I was told by my secretary that the shares of Nozoe's company had risen considerably, from fifty to sixty-five yen. Altogether my five hundred shares were worth 32,500 yen."

"Good show! I also thought about holding some shares myself," said square face.

"It was an exceptional turn of events. I never expected such a steady rise in the price of the stock," said salt-and-pepper hair, scratching his salt-and-pepper head.

"I ought to have seized the opportunity and secured more shares," said bald head regretfully, despite his 32,500 yen windfall.

Takayanagi timidly passed them by. Wishing to express his thanks to Nakano and his wife before leaving, he looked around and found them at the farthest end of the tent. Only with the greatest effort could he approach them, surrounded as they were by black frock coats and multicolored kimonos. Fewer people were at the table now, but hardly any food remained.

"Do you get out much these days?" he heard a voice ask. He turned to see a man of about thirty wearing a ceremonial skirt of thick silk that swept the ground, revealing a pair of white socks and gray-strapped sandals on his feet.

"Yesterday, I was invited by the Tanedas to hunt wild ducks at their villa in Susaki," replied a dark-complexioned man with closely cropped hair.

"It's a bit early for ducks, isn't it?"

"No. The season is ripe for the sport. I got ten, Otaki got seven, and Kase and Yamaguchi got eight each."

"You bagged the most, then?"

"No. Saitō got fifteen."

"Did he?" said ceremonial skirt, looking impressed.

Of his numerous fellow graduates, Takayanagi had met only five or six of them here. Since he did not know them well, he parted from them after an exchange of formal greetings, and without engaging in conversation, but now he felt like he missed them. He looked about but could find no trace of them. They must have gone home. He thought he ought to as well.

Host and guest are one. There is no guest without a host and no host without a guest. It is only for the sake of convenience in our lives that we make a distinction between the two. We think of color and form as separate entities, though neither form nor color can exist independently. We think of technique and concept as separate entities, though in fact they are closely correlated. Once we understand this, we have allowed ourselves to enter a maze; and since life is most important to us, we find it more and more difficult to get out of the labyrinth, created for the sake of convenience in our lives, the deeper we proceed into it. Only when one is emancipated from the desires of life can this bewilderment be overcome. Takayanagi was a man who could not liberate himself from this desire. Consequently, he could not conceive of host and guest separately, obstinately attached to the idea that host is host and guest is guest. Whenever he met a superior guest, he felt attacked by invisible swords on every side. At this garden party Takayanagi felt as if he had taken a lone position against enemy troops.

Takayanagi, who had entered the arch with an uncertain step, must now leave in the same way. Looking back, he saw, through the arch of cedar boughs, the far-away tent grow smaller, and out of it flowed people in fine clothes. Among them must be the young couple.

The young couple was looking for Takayanagi.

"What has become of Takayanagi, I wonder. Have you seem him since he arrived?"

"No. Have you?"

"No. Neither have I."

"Perhaps his has gone home already."

"Perhaps so. But if he were leaving, he ought to have come to us to have a chat."

"Why will he not come where there are other people?"

"What a shame. Such a man of lonely habit is sure to feel awkward. When he feels awkward, he ought to mingle with others, but he withdraws into himself all the more. I am truly sorry for him."

"And to think we invited him to brighten his spirits."

"Today he looked particularly pale."

"I am certain he is not well."

"He looks that way because he lives a solitary life."

While walking along the street, Takayanagi felt a sudden chill.

10

Dōya-sensei, making his long face longer than usual, sat at a round wooden brazier, its exterior made of brown-stained bamboo. A late autumn blast raged outside.

"Dear?" asked his wife, coming in from the next room. She wore a pongee overcoat with its collar sticking up.

"What is it?" he asked, turning toward her. Though he had been at home sitting at his desk all day, he looked like he had been outdoors, exposed to the raging blast.

"Did you sell your manuscript?"

"No, not yet."

"You did say you were expecting in a month or so one or two hundred yen to come in, didn't you?"

"Uhm. That is what I said, but I haven't sold it yet."

"That puts a strain on our finances, doesn't it?"

"Yes, it does. I am strained more than you, and I'm considering what to do."

"And after you have taken such pains and produced three hundred pages . . . ?"

"Not three hundred, but four hundred and thirty-five pages."

"Then why is it that you cannot sell it?"

"It must be due to the present hard times, I suppose."

"*I suppose?!* Can't you think of some way to sell it?"

"When I submitted it to the Nanmeidō publishing house, they said they would publish it provided it had a preface by someone famous. I thought Adachi would be a good choice since he is a university professor, so I asked him to write the preface. Publishing a book is like borrowing money: one needs a guarantor."

"A guarantor is needed to borrow money, but . . .," she said, scratching her head with her index finger, and making her hair, done up in a chignon, tremble. Dōya watched her.

"Nowadays, book publishing is the same as borrowing money. If an author is not trusted by the publisher, the book can be published only through the mutual responsibility of the author and his recommender."

"Oh, you disappoint me. And all that wasted time and energy, working late into the night, time and time again."

"But that is of no concern to a publisher."

"It may be of no concern to them, but it concerns you very much."

"Ha, ha, ha! That it does. And it concerns you as well."

"I am only speaking about the matter because it concerns me."

"Your speaking about it does not change the fact that I have no credit with the publisher."

"What will you do then?"

"That's why I took it to Adachi."

"And Adachi-san said he would write the preface?"

"Yes, he promised he would. So I left my manuscript with him, but afterwards he wrote to say he would have to refuse."

"But why?"

"I do not know why. Perhaps he did not like doing such a thing."

"And you intend to drop the matter there?"

"Yes, if he is unwilling, I cannot force him."

"Well, then, we are in dire straits, I tell you. The money you borrowed through your brother's good offices—repayment is due already."

"I expected to be able to repay the debt with the manuscript fee, but if I cannot sell it then nothing can be done."

"What foolishness! I have no idea why you put yourself out to write it then."

"From your point of view, it may be foolishness," Dōya said, poking at the charcoal in the brazier with a pair of tongs. His wife said nothing. A wintry blast whistled through the house. Holes in the shoji doors to the entranceway made the sound of kites flapping in a storm.

"How long do you intend to stay like this, dear?" asked his wife helplessly.

"I never think about how long to persevere. We may live on like this, provided we can manage to escape starvation."

"Every time we discuss the matter, you say, 'provided we escape starvation.' It may be true we can manage to get by somehow, someway, but the time will come when we can longer stave off creditors."

"Are you really so worried about the matter?"

His wife looked a little indignant.

"But are you not too imprudent? Have you not turned down all teaching positions that would have earned you a comfortable living, and obstinately insisted on living by the pen?"

"You are right. I am determined to live by the pen. You had better resign yourself to the fact."

"If it were possible for us to live a decent life by that means, I would be resigned to it. I am your wife. I will do nothing to interfere with your choice of profession."

"Then there is nothing more to be said about it."

"But we can barely get by as it is."

"Yes, we can."

"You are too much! Do you not see for yourself how much easier it was for you to teach school and how much harder it is to live off your writing? You were an excellent teacher. But you are not cut out for writing."

"How would you know?"

His wife drooped her head, took out of the breast of her kimono a piece of paper, and blew her nose into it.

"It is not I alone, but your brother also is of the same opinion."

"And you believe what my brother says?"

"Why should I not believe him? He is your elder brother, after all. And moreover, he lives very well."

"I see," he said, and carefully smoothed the ashes in the brazier. Finding a two-inch nail covered with ash, he picked it up with the crooked tongs and, opening one of the shoji doors with the other hand, flung it into the garden.

Nothing grew in the garden. Only a decaying banana tree stood with its broad leaves tattered. The surface of the ground was cracked and curling up at the corners like straw matting. Dōya-sensei looked at the ground and said to himself, "The wind is blowing hard."

"Why don't you ask Adachi-san once again to write the preface?"

"It will not do to ask him again, if he is not inclined to do it."

"Your way of thinking is what gets us in trouble. An important person is not likely to consent to such a request so readily."

"An important person? Adachi?"

"You are an important person in your own right, but he is a university professor. There is no harm in entreating him again."

"I see. Then on your instructions I will entreat him once again. By the way, what time is it now? Dear me! I'm late. I must hurry to the office to read the proofs. Bring me my split skirt trousers."

Dōya-sensei put on his usual narrow-striped skirt of coarse silk and went out into the raging blast. The clock in the sitting room struck two.

An old haiku says, "One by one thoughts come to mind only to disintegrate like charcoal burned to ash." The wife probably did not know it. She went to the brazier in Dōya's room and began leveling the ashes with the tongs, drawing a circle because the brazier was round in shape. If it were a square one, she would arrange the ashes in a square. A woman thinks that what is given is correct, and that to live without friction and contradiction is a virtue. Whether she is given an octagonal or hexagonal brazier, she will continue to smooth the ashes to conform to the shape of the brazier. She has no discernment to do otherwise.

Neither standing nor sitting, she crouched on her heels with her knees touching the rim of the brazier. She does not sit because this is not her usual seat; she does not stand because she cannot think while standing. Both her posture and her thoughts were unresolved.

On reflection, it was wrong to have gotten married. Life was so much easier and more interesting when she was a girl. If someone had told her that this is what married life was like, she would have reconsidered. Seeing how she had been loved by her parents, and taking it for granted that she would be loved all the more by her husband because their bond would "endure even to the next life," and assured by her parents that she would be loved dearly by her future husband, she left home, never to return. And having left home, she could never go back. Even if she could go back, neither her mother nor her father was living. Her desire to be loved was misguided, and those who used to love her were gone.

Dōya-sensei's wife began poking at the pieces of charcoal with the fire tongs, removing the ash from the red embers. Even if the charcoal was reduced to ash, she could rebuild the mound one piece at a time. But once the charcoal has disintegrated, it cannot return to its original form. Perhaps unaware of this simple fact, she continued to poke at the embers.

Looking back now, she realized that she had gotten married with a wrong view about her future. She became a wife for her own sake, never thinking for a moment that it was for the sake of her husband. For the sake of her happiness alone, she drank nuptial cups. While praying for the happiness of their daughter alone, her parents listened to the recitation of the customary auspicious passage from the noh drama, *Takasago*. All her expectations, however, had been betrayed. If she could tell her parents about the recent conduct of her husband, they would be indignant and call his behavior outrageous. She too was secretly angry with him.

Dōya took it for granted that it was a wife's duty to take care of her husband. That is what he wanted to tell her. But she is the weaker vessel, younger in years, and should be taken care of by him. She ought to be cared for by him more than he is to be cared for by her. She tells him to behave as she wants him to, but he has never taken her advice. Domestic life is the life of the wife. But in Dōya's view, it should be centered on the husband. That is the cause of discord in their home. She wonders whether all husbands in the world are like Dōya. If that were the case, fewer and fewer women would get married. But judging from the fact that the number of marriages is not decreasing, most other husbands must be behaving as they ought to. Realizing that she alone in the wide world is miserable in this way, she cannot but be pessimistic about her life. But once she had entered into marriage, she could not leave her husband. Considering that Dōya will ever remain as he is, she will never be able to feel like a real wife to him to her dying day. But she must do something. Unless she succeeds in molding her husband's character to her liking, her life will not be worth living. Meditating on these things, she poked at the charcoal in the brazier. The wind howled strong enough to blow down the withered banana tree in the garden.

A visitor called at the front door. Opening the sliding shoji door to the entranceway, she stuck out her cold head to see Dōya's elder brother standing there, and she cried out in surprise.

The elder brother is an officer in a company, the president of which is Nakano's father. Taking off a long Inverness in the hall, he entered the drawing room.

"The wind is picking up," he said, sitting down on a chintz cushion, and rubbing his balding forehead.

"So good of you to come in spite of the weather."

"I left the office early today."

"You were on your way home?"

"No, I went home to change clothes before coming here. I cannot feel comfortable in my Western suit when I sit on the floor." He wore a silk kimono and a grey overcoat of Hakata fabric.

"Has he gone out?"

"Yes, he left a little while ago. He will be back before long. Please make yourself comfortable," she said, placing the brazier nearer to him.

"Please do not trouble yourself for me. It has indeed turned cold," he said, warming his hands over the fire.

"You must be very busy, what with the year-end round the corner."

"Thank you for your sympathy. The year-end causes me such headaches every time. Ha, ha, ha!" He laughed, but people do not laugh only when amused.

"But to be so busy must be a good thing."

"Well, yes, I manage to make ends meet. By the way, I suppose Dōya is the same as always."

"Thank you for asking. He keeps himself busy."

"Excellent, no? Ha, ha, ha. He is a difficult fellow, isn't he, O-masa-san. I never thought he would be so incorrigible."

"I am sorry he worries you so. I speak to him, of course, but he will never listen to me, despising me as a foolish woman. I am utterly at a loss with what to do with him."

"I quite understand, for he will pay no attention to what I say to him either. But when we are together, I cannot refrain from advising him from time to time."

"As well you should. Everyone seems to be aware of our predicament."

"If he were still living in the country, it would be different, but now, living near him, I felt it was my duty as his brother to intercede, whether he likes it or not. And the consequence? He remains aloof. He's an eccentric, he is. If he could have modestly carried out his teaching duties, but no, he collided with school authorities or the public everywhere he went."

"That temperament of his always worried me. You don't know how much grief it caused me."

"I can well understand. I sympathize with you."

"Thank you for your understanding. I'm afraid we have been quite troublesome."

"Even since coming to Tokyo, he might have secured a better occupation than his present drudgery. But each time I bring up the subject, he turns a deaf ear. I would not object to his intransigence, provided he could find a respectable position for himself."

"I myself have complained to him to the same effect often enough, but to no avail."

"Yet, in times of emergency, he comes to me for help."

"I am so sorry."

"I do not at all mean to blame you, but I do blame him. He is reckless, after all. What kind of man would still continue to engage in hack writing seven or eight years after graduation? Look at his friend Adachi: he is now a famous university professor, is he not?"

"But in his own mind, Dōya believes himself to be great in his own way."

"Great in his own way! Ha, ha, ha! However great he may be in his own opinion, it is meaningless unless others recognize him as such."

"Recently I have been begun to think that there might be something wrong with his mind."

"What can I say. I hear he is constantly attacking rich people. Sheer nonsense. What is interesting in that? It is both unprofitable and disreputable. For all his pains, he only makes himself notorious."

"I only wish he would listen to what people say."

"What is worse, he is vexatious. Actually, I was a bit embarrassed at the office today. My section chief pulled me aside and said, 'I hear Shirai Dōya is your brother. That man is expressing some extreme thoughts in his articles, attacking the rich and other people. This must stop. You would do well to admonish him.' And he said other things in the same harsh language."

"Oh, dear me! I wonder how he came to know such things."

"Well, business firms have private investigators in their employment, you see."

"Oh, is that so?"

"Whatever sentiments Dōya may express, I am sure the public will take no notice of a nonentity such as he. But now that I have been warned by my boss, I can no longer ignore the matter."

"You are quite right to think so."

"As a matter of fact, I have come today to discuss the matter with him."

"I am sorry; he has gone out."

"It is more convenient this way. Consulting with you alone is enough. On my way home I was considering the matter from various angles. But what is your idea?"

"I should like you to speak seriously to him and try to persuade him to become a teacher again. What do you say to that?"

"If he could become a teacher again, that would be satisfactory. You would be happy and I would be relieved. However, he is not one to follow other's advice unquestioningly."

"No, he is not. I'm afraid he would not listen to you either."

"In my evaluation, he is beyond advice. But I do have a plan to induce him to give up writing for magazines and newspapers on his own accord, and to urge him to return to teaching."

"I would be grateful to you. What shall we do to bring about your plan?"

"What became of that book he was writing?"

"It still remains in manuscript form."

"He has not sold it?"

"No, he cannot sell it anywhere. Every publisher has rejected it."

"All the better that he has not sold it."

"What do you mean?"

"Its failure better suits our purpose. His loan of one hundred yen, which I was guarantor, is due soon, is it not?"

"Yes, on the fifteenth."

"Today is the eleventh. Twelfth, thirteenth, fourteenth—there remain only four more days before it is due."

"Yes."

"I plan to squeeze the money out of him. I can confess the truth to you now: I affixed my seal to the note as guarantor, but I was also the lender. Otherwise, he might not cooperate. Now we can force his hand. He has no other means of repayment, has he?"

"None that I can think of."

"Excellent. Then I can begin to apply pressure. No, I will just watch in silence. The creditor, the actual name on the loan, will come to collect. You must of course feign ignorance, and keep a dispassionate attitude, no matter what he says. Not a single word of sympathy. However stubborn he may be, eventually he will have to come to me for help. When he humbles himself before me, I will take control. Do you see? Then I will say to him, 'Now that you resort to me for help, you must take my advice in return for my help, otherwise I will do nothing for you.' He cannot possibly say 'No.' Then I will say, 'Think of your wife, O-Masa. How she suffers to make ends meet. This is no time to indulge your demagoguery in magazines. Change your heart completely and follow a modest and harmless profession. If you are interested in becoming a teacher again, I can make introductions for you.' That is how I will carry it off. And he will have to do as we say. What do you think?"

"You cannot imagine what a relief it would be to me."

"Shall I put him to the test?"

"By all means, please do."

"Then it's decided. Just one more thing. On my way home from the office today, as I was passing the Seikikan Hall in Kanda, I was surprised to see a certain advertisement."

"What kind of advertisement?"

"For a public lecture. It is not the lecture that's important but the lecturer. The advertisement said the lecturer was Dōya."

"Oh! I knew nothing of it!"

"It had an interesting title, printed in large letters, "My Appeal to Today's Youth." What is he thinking? I can hardly imagine any young person curious enough to go hear him. It could be dangerous. We don't know what he might say. Having just been cautioned by my boss, I immediately telephoned the office and reported the matter. I did all I could. If possible, we must prevent him from lecturing."

"I wonder what he intends to speak about. He is going to make a nuisance of himself."

"He is certain to say something radical again. One hopes his lecture would proceed without incident, but if he speaks trivialities, his words are irrevocable. We must do all we can to stop him."

"But how can we stop him?"

"If we tell him not to give his lecture, he will ignore us because he is obstinate. We need a strategy."

"But what strategy shall we use?"

"Let me see. Tomorrow about the time the lecture is to begin, I shall send a messenger on the pretext that I have to see him about something urgent. How about that?"

"Well, yes. But I doubt if he will come meekly."

"Your doubt is reasonable. He may not come. If he proves intractable, there is nothing we can do."

The early winter day came to a close. Dōya-sensei came home through the storm.

11

A raw wind continued to blow, as if to render every moist thing into something desiccated and hard like dried salmon.

"A messenger has come from your brother," said Dōya's wife, handing a letter to her husband. Dōya remained seated but turned around to take it.

"Is he waiting for an answer?"

"Yes."

Dōya opened the envelope and read the letter. He rolled it up and put it back in the envelope, saying nothing.

"Is it something urgent?"

"Uhm," he said, grinding his ink stick, and rapidly writing a reply.

"Important business?"

"What? Wait a moment. I'm almost finished."

"Here." He addressed the note of five or six lines and handed it to her. The wife, calling the maid and giving the note to her, stood motionless.

"What was that about?"

"I don't know what it was about. I was asked to come to discuss business of some kind."

"You are going, aren't you?"

"No, I cannot. You may go, if you like."

"I? I cannot go."

"Why?"

"Because I'm a woman."

"Better a woman go than no one go at all."

"But in the note you were asked to come, weren't you?"

"But I am not able to go."

"Why?"

"I have to go out now."

"If it is the magazine office, surely you can take a day off."

"This is not editing work. I have to give a lecture."

"A public lecture? You are giving a public lecture?"

"Yes, I am. I see no reason for you to be so surprised."

"The wind is blowing so hard today. I think you should give it up."

"Ha, ha, ha! If my lecture was something that could be canceled by bad weather, I would never have undertaken it in the first place."

"But you would do well not to say anything untoward."

"Untoward? What do you mean?"

"I mean it would be to your advantage not to give the lecture."

"I see nothing to my advantage in refraining from speaking in public."

"There might be undesirable consequences."

"What strange things you say. Who told you that I should not give my lecture?"

"No one told me that. But you must consider that you've received an urgent message from your brother delivered by messenger. It would be a breach of etiquette not to comply."

"Then I should have to cancel my lecture."

"Can't you cancel it by explaining you have an emergency?"

"I cannot cancel at the last minute."

"Then do you mean to say that your obligation to your brother can be canceled at the last minute?"

"I never said that. But my lecture is an earlier commitment. Moreover, today's lecture is no ordinary lecture. It is rather a lecture to save people."

"To save people? Whom are you going to save?"

"A person in our magazine office was arrested for instigating the recent riot against the introduction of the electric tramway. His family, as a result, has fallen on hard times. And out of sympathy for their misery, we organized this lecture with the intent of giving the ticket sales to the poor family."

"Undoubtedly it is a splendid idea to save the man's family. But if you are mistaken for a socialist, I fear undesirable consequences will follow."

"I do not care if I am mistaken for a socialist. Whether a nationalist or a socialist, one should follow the way of justice."

"But suppose you end up like the man in question? Then I must suffer the same fate as his wife? You are welcome to save others, but you ought to have a little consideration for me as well. This is too much!"

Dōya-sensei was plunged deep in thought for a while, and then, standing up from his desk, said, "There can be no possibility of such nonsense! We no longer live under the Tokugawa regime."

Putting on his usual split skirt trousers, in a matter of minutes he was prepared for his lecture. He went into the entranceway. The wind was blowing as strongly as before. Dōya-sensei's form disappeared into the storm.

The lecture was held in the Seikikan Hall during the middle of the storm.

Four speakers were on the program, and an audience of less than three hundred had assembled, most of them students. Among them was Takayanagi Shūsaku, Bachelor of Arts. He came walking through the blast with his face wrapped in a muffler, coughing from time to time. He paid the ten-sen admission and went up to the gallery. The large auditorium was far from full, and all the vacant seats made him feel lonely. He took a seat on the southern side, looking for warmth. The lecture soon began.

"Patronage of the literary profession is demanded only by writers who cannot manage to be self-reliant. Properly speaking, patronage belongs to the age of aristocracy; it is a disgrace to speak of it in the present age of individualism and equality. A writer worthy of the name should not stoop to patronage but should make society pay the proper reward for his craft." The speaker left the stage. The audience applauded. Not far from Takayanagi, two students in splashed-pattern overcoats were talking.

"Was that speaker Kuroda Tōyō?"

"Yes."

"Funny looking man. I expected him to be better looking."

"Perhaps with patronage his looks might improve."

Takayanagi looked at the two students. The two students looked at Takayanagi.

"Hey!"

"What?"

"What is he staring at?"

"Who does he think he is?"

"Who is up next? Look! Look! There he is!"

"He's a skinny one. How did he make it here without getting blown away?"

The skinny Dōya-sensei, in his cotton clothing, appeared on stage. He had braved the elements, walking as straight as a needle. Exposed to the dry wind, he looked like an old withered gourd. The sound of hands clapping filled the air. The clapping of hands is not necessarily the same as applause. Takayanagi alone sat silently and adjusted his collar.

"Man is a link between the past and the future."

Dōya-sensei began abruptly. The audience was taken by surprise. No one started his lecture this way.

"Those who carry over the past into the future are called conservative; those who save the future from the past are called progressive."

The audience was more puzzled than before. Among the audience of three hundred were those who came to jeer Dōya-sensei. Given the slightest opportunity, they would laugh him off the stage. Like sumo wrestlers in a ring, they watched for a chance to take advantage of their opponent. They were poised like a snake ready to strike. In Dōya-sensei's vision there was nothing but the Way.

"If you say you have no past in yourself, you may as well say you have no parents. If you say you have no future in yourself, you may as well say you have no capacity to beget children. One's standpoint should be clear from this. Either to live for your parents, to live for your children, or to live for yourself: your mission in life can be only one of these three alternatives."

The audience remained dumbfounded. Or, perhaps, they were shrouded in mist. Takayanagi listened approvingly.

"The Renaissance, in a general sense, was a great age that existed for the sake of its parents. The late eighteenth-century Gothic Revival, again in a general sense, was a small age that also existed for the sake of its parents. But at the same time, it gave birth to the Romanticism of the school of Sir Walter Scott, an age that existed for its children as well. As for an age that existed for is own sake, its best example is the age of Elizabethan literature. As for individuals who have lived for their own sake, we could mention Ibsen, Meredith, Nietzsche, and Browning. Christians live for the sake of Christ, who lived in ancient times; Christians therefore live for the sake of the father. Confucians live for the sake of Confucius, who lived in ancient times; Confucians therefore live for the sake of the father."

"We get the point," someone yelled from the audience.

"No, you still do not understand what I mean," said Dōya-sensei. The audience broke into laughter.

"Does a lined kimono exist for the sake of the unlined kimono or for the sake of a cotton-padded one? Or does it exist for its own sake?" he asked, looking out over the audience. His remark was too witty to laugh at, too comical to take seriously. The audience did not know how to react.

"A difficult question indeed. I do not know the answer myself," he said with a straight face. The audience laughed once more.

"That problem may safely remain unsolved. But for what do we ourselves live? This is a problem that must be solved. The Meiji Era has lasted for forty years. Forty years is not a short time. It may seem that the Meiji enterprise has successfully come to a close."

"No! No!" someone shouted in English.

"I am in agreement with that person who said 'No.' I was expecting such a response."

The audience laughed again.

"No, really, I was waiting for it. "

The audience laughed a third time.

"I have said forty years is not a short space of time. Granted, they may seem a long time to those who have lived through them. But will that span of time seem long to those who live in the years after Meiji? The lens of a telescope is a mere inch in diameter, but viewed from the top of Mount Atago, the entire Shinagawa coast fits into that one-inch diameter lens. Those to whom the forty years of Meiji seem long are the ones actively involved in Meiji, but the next generation will think of them on a much-reduced scale. Seen from the distant future, Meiji's forty years will be but a moment. What can be accomplished in a moment?" Dōya rapped the table, surprising the audience.

"Our politicians believe they have done a great deal. Our scholars are confident they have made great strides. Our men of business and the military think they have accomplished much. All of them believe they have done much, but that is their own estimation. With their heads stuck in the atmosphere of Meiji's forty years, they overestimate their own achievements. But what can be accomplished in a mere moment?"

No one laughed now.

"People say, 'We are living in the fortieth year of Meiji, but Japan has failed to produce a Shakespeare or a Goethe during this time.' Because they think forty years a long time, they speak such foolishness. But what can be accomplished in a mere moment?"

"Just wait. They'll come!" someone shouted.

"Yes, they may appear. But the man of genius has not yet emerged. In a word—," he paused mid-sentence. The house waited in silence.

"The forty year span of Meiji forms the first stage of Meiji Enlightenment. To put it another way, we today are living in an age of Enlightenment with no past. As a consequence, we are not living in order to communicate the past. But time flows without stopping. There is no age without a past. Gentlemen, do not misunderstand me. Of course we have a past. But our past is a decrepit past or an infantile past. We have no past to look to for a model. The forty-year span of Meiji is a period without precedent."

Some faces in the audience looked skeptical.

"There is none so free as he who is born into a society without a precedent. I, for one, congratulate you on having been born into this society without a precedent."

The sound of "Here! Here!" went up from different parts of the hall.

"Your hasty assent is rather embarrassing to me. Those born into a society without precedent ought to create their own precedent. Those who enjoy unlimited freedom are already limited by freedom itself. How to make use of this freedom is your responsibility, as well as your privilege. Gentlemen! If you do not maintain high ideals, your freedom is only depravity."

Pausing, Dōya-sensei placed both hands on the table and looked over the entire audience. Amazement prevailed over the scene as if a thunderbolt had fallen in the midst of the auditorium.

"Let me take an individual case as an illustration of what I mean. One who looks back on his past is a grey-haired man. A young man has no past to look back on. Having a bright future ahead of him, he does not need to yearn for his past. The age we now live in is an age of youth, an age not yet old enough to long for the past. In politics, it is not an age to look back on Marquis Itō or Marquis Yamagata. In business, it is not an age to look back on Baron Shibusawa or Baron Iwasaki."

"Big talk!" exclaimed Takayanagi's neighbor, the Satsuma splashed pattern. Takayanagi felt indignant.

"In literature, it is not an age to look back on Ozaki Kōyō or Higuchi Ichiyō. All these people did not live to be a precedent for you. They lived in order to produce you! To use my previous figure of speech, these people lived for the sake of the future. Their existence is for posterity. But you must live for your own sake. Those living in the beginning of an age must be prepared to live for posterity; those living in the middle of an age must be determined to live for themselves; those living in the end of an age must be resigned to living for the sake of the father. Meiji has now lasted for forty years; we must regard those years as a beginning period. If such is the case, the youth of today owe it to themselves to develop to their full stature so as to shape the middle period of Meiji. You need not look behind you; you need not care what lies ahead. All you have to do is realize yourself as far as it lies in you. Nothing in life can be more delightful than your mission!" A ripple of excitement resounded through the audience.

"Why can the beginning period furnish no precedent? Because it is the most disorderly and irregular period. It is a period in which fortune plays a predominant part. Those who won fame in the beginning period, who rose in social position, who made fortunes, and who built enterprises did not necessarily succeed and prosper by virtue of their own talents. To succeed except by one's own capacity would be shameful to an honest man. In this regard, those living in the middle period are far happier than those living in the beginning period. Happier are they for they have greater difficulties in accomplishing things; happier are they for their difficulties leave no room for luck to play a part; happier are they for, despite their difficulties, they have the leisure to go where they please in accordance with their capacities, and have a path of development. In the late period all things become rigidly fixed. People living in such a period cannot behave freely but can only follow in the footsteps of those who have gone before. When people become bound by tradition and grow decadent, catastrophe will set in. Unless a change occurs, society becomes fossilized. But human nature cannot bear fossilization, so it will cause a catastrophe of its own accord. This is called a revolution.

"So far, I have tried to explain your position in the world of Meiji. Occupying such a happy position, you must cultivate the ideals worthy of this happiness."

This point marked a departure in his lecture. The audience remained silent, apparently no longer inclined to jeer at the speaker.

"Ideals are the soul of man. The soul, being formless, cannot be grasped. We can only conjecture what kind of soul a man has by observing its revelations in his behavior. It is regrettable that contemporary youth cannot discover any ideals. They may seek them in the past and not find them; they may seek them in the present and not find them. Can you find your ideals in your parents at home?"

Some in attendance looked nonplussed, but remained silent.

"Can you find your ideals in your teachers at school?

"No! No!

"Can you find your ideals in the so-called gentleman of society?

"No! No!

"As a matter of fact, you have no ideals. At home you despise your parents; at school you despise your teachers; in society you despise the gentleman. Your ability to despise these people is a critical power in you. But in order to despise them, you must possess higher ideals than theirs. Despising others while lacking ideals yourself is depravity. The youth of today are becoming more and more depraved by the day."

The audience looked restless. Someone murmured, "What churlishness!" Dōya-sensei proudly looked down at the audience.

"There are those who sing the praises of the English way of life. I pity them, for they only expose their own lack of ideals. Though the youth of Japan may be getting more and more depraved by the day, I believe they have not yet fallen so low. An ideal is the soul of one's life. It must come from within. A slavish mind can never entertain a noble ideal. Japanese who are dazzled by Western ideals are slavish. When they not only wallow in their slavery but vie with one another over degrees of slavery, how can their minds generate ideals of their own?

"Gentlemen! Your ideals must spring forth from deep within. Only when your knowledge and opinions have been transformed into your flesh and blood and have become a part of your soul will you have formed your own ideals. Borrowing from other nations will prove of no use."

Placing one fist on the table, Dōya-sensei paused, looking as if to challenge the audience to jeer. His poor clothing—dirty black cotton overcoat, threadbare split skirt trousers—had now ceased to attract attention. The wind howled noisily.

"Those who have ideals know the Way to take. Those who have great ideals walk the great Way. They are not like lost children. Whatever may happen, they must follow the Way. They could not stray from the Way if they wanted to, for their soul is always directing their course.

"Some of you may want to ask how far a man should go along the Way. Of course he should go as far as he can, for that is the purpose of life. No one knows how long he is destined to live. He knows not the length of his own life, much less can others know it. Even the greatest doctor cannot predict the span of human years. Only after having lived out your years can you begin to number your days. Only ex post facto can one assert that he has lived for eighty years. Even if convinced that you will live for eighty years, no one will take you for your word until you have proved your conviction by accomplishing the fact. Therefore, one should not speak of such things. The same applies to those who, having received the revelation of their ideals, march toward their goal. It is beyond their calculation how much they can accomplish in realizing their ideals. To judge the future based on the past is as silly as to assume that because you lived a certain number of years in the past you are bound to live for as many years in the future. It is a speculation at best. All people that calculate on success in life are speculators!"

The Satsuma splash pattern next to Takayanagi assumed a quizzical expression.

"Society is a battleground. Civilized society is a bloodless battleground. Our patriots of forty years ago accomplished the great work of the Meiji Restoration, risking death. The risks you must brave may prove greater than theirs. The bloodless battleground is more dreadful, more tragic than the battleground of thunderous guns and glinting bayonets. You must be prepared for that. You must be better prepared than those patriots in the Imperial cause. You must be prepared for certain death. Those who think their society is a peaceful society, who expect success without struggle, are far more morally impoverished than those who fall down to die on their way to realizing their ideals.

"While marching on your way, you will have to drive off those who put up obstacles in the way. While fighting with them, you will experience greater pains and hardships in your inner life than those that the patriots suffered. Today the wind blows hard, as it did yesterday. We are having unsettled weather these days. But it is nothing compared to the moral uncertainty you may have ahead of you!"

Dōya-sensei looked out at the street through the windows rattling in the blast. A gust of wind blew up the dust in the street, dashing it against the rooftops, and then dispersed it in the open sky.

"Gentlemen! What power you have I cannot know. Neither can you yourself know. Our posterity alone can decide the question. Not until you have marched along the road to your ideals as far as you can and have dropped dead in your tracks, only at that moment can you learn the extent of your own power. You must be content to live in the works you will have accomplished. It is frivolous to try to go down in history on the merit of your name."

Takayanagi felt somewhat ashamed of himself. He thought Dōya's sparkling gaze was cast on him.

"Ideals vary from one individual to another. We cultivate learning. For a scholar, what are his ideals?"

No response came from the audience.

"Whatever a scholar's ideals may be, they have nothing to do with wealth."

Laughter rose from five or six places in the hall. Dōya-sensei's lack of wealth was obvious to all who noticed his dress. Dōya-sensei extended the sleeves of his overcoat with his hands and examined first one sleeve and then the other. The weave of the black cotton fabric was full of sand.

"Quite dirty, I see," Dōya said with perfect composure.

The entire audience burst into laughter. But it was not the laughter of ridicule. Dōya-sensei had crushed the laughter of ridicule with the laughter of good will.

"The other day I had a visit from a friend, a man dedicated to learning, who said that now that he has a wife and child he must make a fortune, saving as much money as he could, so that he might give his child the best possible education. And he asked, 'But what is the best way to build sufficient savings?'

"No question can be more stupid than 'How can one make money by means of learning?' The purpose behind learning is to become a scholar. It is not to become wealthy. Trying to contrive ways to make money through learning is kin to going to the North Pole to snare a tiger."

The audience seemed somewhat disturbed.

"Generally speaking, people have a grossly mistaken idea of the relationship between work and money. They think that if one acquires a respectable amount of learning, one may expect to earn a correspondingly large income. But that logic is entirely fallacious. Learning is a mechanism that alienates one from wealth. If it's money you want, you have to become entrepreneurs or merchants. Scholars and businessmen have nothing in common. Scholars who cultivate learning for the sake of money are like young men who become shop-boys for the sake of scholarship."

"Really now?" someone ejaculated. The audience roared. Dōya-sensei calmly waited for the laughter to subside.

"Therefore, if you would know of learning, you must ask a scholar; if you would have money, you must go and inquire of a merchant."

"It's money I want!" someone interrupted. Dōya could not tell who.

"I'm sure that you do," he said and proceeded.

"To be learned, that is to say, to understand the reason behind things, on the one hand, and to be liberally provided with means to satisfy one's material desires, that is, to be wealthy, on the other, are not only independent of each other, they are mutually exclusive. To be learned is to be lacking money. To be bent on making money is to remain without learning. Scholars lack money but have reason. Merchants lack reason but make money."

Dōya-sensei paused for about twenty seconds, expecting someone to make a remark, but no one dared.

"Ignoring this fact and assuming that money and reason go together, people commit the height of folly. Yet this folly is almost universal. They believe that because a wealthy man is respected by the public, he must possess reason and culture. But the fact is because he has no time for culture, he is able to amass a fortune. Nature is impartial; she does not permit a man to become cultured as well as rich. In disregard of this fact, rich people flatter themselves. . . . "

"Here! Here!" said one. "You're jealous!" said another. Still others hissed.

"The rich, standing high in society, fancy that they are respected by the public, that they among all others possess the highest powers of reason, and that everyone including scholars ought to bow down to them. They are to be pitied, for their complacency proves their lack of culture."

Takayanagi's eyes shone with excitement, and blood rushed to his cheeks.

"Even if we may condone the self-satisfaction of the rich as incorrigible, we cannot but declare the public's injudiciousness in accepting rich people's self-estimation. People often say, 'Since that man holds such a high social position and possesses considerable property, he must be proportionately wise.' But on the contrary, that man is decidedly unwise, because he succeeded in rising high in society by acquiring a large fortune."

Takayanagi, forgetting the pain in his chest, cried, "Here! Here!" and clapped his hands. The Satsuma splashed pattern at his side cleared his throat with a sarcastic, "Ahem!"

"There are various ways to determine how people achieve high positions in society. In the first place, some people get there by culture. Second, because they belong to good families. Third, because of their talents in the arts. And, finally, by money. Most people of high positions in society get there by this way, money. There are these distinct criteria for high social positions which people get mixed up, equating the social position of men due to their wealth with the social position of men due to their learning. They are blind to the truth."

"Ahem! Ahem!" Scattered voices arose from the hall. Takayanagi pressed his lips together, breathing audibly through the nose.

"Those whose market price is determined by their wealth have no credit to their name other than money. Money by definition is valuable, and the rich gain respect on account of their possession of the valuable. That is well and good. There is no objection to make. But in other fields outside of money, they have no claim of respect. They are not to comingle as equals with those who stand high on the social scale by virtue of qualifications other than money. If they could comingle, then scholars might enter the domain of the rich and lay claim to the same authority and honor as the moneyed class. But the rich would not allow such a thing. Not content to be confined genteelly to their own domain, they would trespass into others' as well. This desire of the rich is proof of their ignorance."

Half rising from his seat, Takayanagi clapped his hands. Imitation being human nature, a wave of clapping sounds filled the hall. The sneering faction remained quiet, overwhelmed by the majority.

"Money is reward for labor. The more you work, the more money you make. In this regard, society is fair, thus far. (No, unfair circumstances do exist: speculators make money without labor.) But if we pursue the matter further, is higher labor accompanied by higher reward? Gentlemen, I ask you. Failing to get an answer, I must give my own. The reward for labor is determined by whether the given form of labor will serve the immediate interests of society. Consequently, a schoolteacher's salary is smaller than a petty shopkeeper's income. The higher the purpose of one's work, the smaller its monetary reward, regardless of the prospect that the work is likely to promote the future interests of the community, of the nation, or of humanity. Therefore, it is not the nature of labor, of high purpose or low, that decides the amount of reward. The quality of the labor does not affect the distribution of money. Hence, it does not follow that the rich have performed a higher form of labor. You cannot evaluate a man's worth according to the amount of money he has acquired."

Dōya paused after his passionate delivery to observe how his remarks had been received by the audience. A printed speech is a lifeless thing. Dōya intended to adapt his lecture to the response of the audience. But they were quieter than he expected.

"It is wrong for the rich to be haughty because of wealth. It is wrong for them to believe they are warranted to rival the learned on account of their wealth. It is wrong for them to expect cultured people to bow down to them. —Well, let them stop to think for a moment. However rich they may be, they must defer to a doctor if they fall ill. Can they make an infusion of gold coins and cure themselves by drinking it?"

Three or four people snorted at this remark, earnestly comic. Dōya took notice.

"Is it not so? An infusion of gold coins cannot possibly cure even loose bowels. So the rich must bow to their doctors. The doctors, in turn, bow to gold."

Dōya-sensei grinned. The audience smiled agreeably.

"This is quite all right. Doctors may well bow to gold. But the rich are inadmissible. Knowing full well that they must bow to doctors, the rich do not know to bow to the learned and the wise in matters concerning taste, culture, or character. On the contrary, they want to make the latter bow down to them by the power of money. There is truth in the proverb, 'the blind fear no snakes,' isn't there?"

The speaker's tone suddenly turned conversational.

"The learned and the wise promote the happiness of society through their learning and wisdom, just as the rich contribute to material welfare through their wealth. Therefore, though in different fields, they maintain a solid, inviolable status in society.

"When the learned become involved in money matters, they leave their own domain and enter another's territory, so naturally they must bow to the rich. In the same way, on problems beyond financial affairs—taste or literature, life or society—the rich must come to scholars. Now suppose a dispute arises between the learned and the wealthy. If the dispute is over money matters, scholars are plainly helpless. When it comes to disputes over problems of life, or morality, or society, however, the rich should realize they have no voice in such matters, and should humbly submit to the decision of scholars. The Iwasakis may be mighty enough to overwhelm scholars by building many a villa, but they are like helpless babes in the face of problems of life and society. If they should fancy that by building villas of a hundred thousand *tsubo* in the four quarters of the capital they have succeeded in humiliating all the learned in the land, they would be as silly as those who fancy that by building Ryōunkaku, the twelve-story pavilion, they have disturbed the heavenly sages."

Dōya's attitude and witticisms dumbfounded the audience. Takayanagi alone could not refrain from shouting and clapping.

"When merchants make use of their capital to get more money, they remain in their proper field, and no outsider has a right to interfere. But when they use their money not in business but in other fields of human endeavor, they ought to seek advice from the wise. Otherwise, they may be brewing social evils unconsciously. Part of the money in the hands of the rich is consistently abused in this way. It all stems from the fact that, whereas they are masters of great wealth, they are not masters of virtue and the arts. It all stems from the fact that they have not learned to honor scholars. It all stems from the fact that, despite warnings of the latter, they cannot understand the significance of what they are told. An evil committed never fails to return to the perpetrator. The time will come when they will be obliged to listen to the words of scholars and men of letters. The time will come when they will no longer be able to hold their social positions, unless they listen."

The audience broke into thunderous applause all at once. Takayanagi, in spite of his consumption, clapped the loudest. He had never heard such a soul-gratifying speech in his life. He felt reward for his pains in coming here, walking through the storm with his head half wrapped in his muffler. Dōya-sensei stood erect on the platform like a prophet. The autumn wind rattled the rafters.

12

"Are you any better?" he asked, sitting down at the foot of the bed.

In the six-mat room, the mats were old and frayed to the point that, if struck with the hand, dust motes would be visible even at night. A medicine bottle and a thermometer lay on a round tray of Miyajima manufacture. Coming home from the lecture, Takayanagi suffered a long-apprehended lung hemorrhage.

"I feel better today," he replied, sitting up in bed, and covering the lower half of his body with a sleeved coverlet.

Nakano took a Russian-leather cigarette case out of a sleeve of his Oshima pongee kimono, but then caught himself.

"I shouldn't smoke here," he said, and dropped the case into his sleeve again.

"Never mind. A little smoke is not going to affect me one way or the other," the patient said sadly.

"You are wrong. The incipient stage requires the most care. You have to start taking better care of yourself now. Yesterday I went to see your doctor and asked about you. He said it's nothing serious. Did he come, by the way?"

"He came this morning. He told me to keep warm."

"Yes, you should keep warm. It is rather cold in this room," Nakano said, looking around forlornly.

"And you had better have the maid or someone repaper the shoji doors. The wind will blow in and make the room colder."

"Repaper the shoji?"

"Perhaps you should go somewhere for a change of air."

"The doctor also advised me to do so."

"Then you must go by all means. Did he say so this morning?"

"Yes."

"And what did you say?"

"I said nothing. It is not a question I could readily answer."

"You had better go then."

"Yes, I know, but I cannot go without money," Takayanagi said with a cheerless face, looking down at his knees. The edge of his flannel inner kimono protruded two inches from the gassed-cotton outer kimono. The two kimonos appeared to have been sewn separately without regard to measurement.

"Don't worry about that. I will take care of things."

Takayanagi raised his dry eyes from his knees and looked at Nakano's happy face. Takayanagi's reply would depend on the expression on this face.

"I will manage somehow. Why do you look at me with those eyes?"

Takayanagi suddenly realized that his heart had been looking through the windows of his eyes.

"Am I to borrow the money from you?"

"No, you don't have to."

"Then are you going to give it to me?"

"Whichever you prefer. You need not concern yourself."

"I don't like to borrow money."

"Then don't borrow it."

"But I don't like receiving it as a gift, either."

"You are a difficult man. Why do you have to make things so complicated? In our college days, do you not remember you would often ask for a loan or ask me to treat you to Western-style dinners?

"In those days I was not ill."

"If you used to make use of my money then, why not now, when you need it more? Nobody is going to blame you for receiving my help. Friends ought to help each other in need."

"That is the argument from the helping friend."

"Is there something about me that upsets you?"

"Nothing at all. I am very grateful to you."

"Then why don't you accept my offer with good grace? You wear the spectacles of pessimism, which make you find the world unpleasant. But must we feel pain because you willfully find us unpleasant creatures?"

Takayanagi said nothing for a while. Perhaps he was living to make the world uncomfortable. He had never been liked wherever he went. But now that his days were numbered, he did not want to owe anyone a debt of gratitude. If he were born to make the world uncomfortable, it would be insignificant to please a single human being, that is, Nakano. If he were destined to make the world uncomfortable, it would be better to die as soon as possible.

"I am sorry to decline your kind offer, but I will not go anywhere for change of air. Please forgive me."

"There you are being unreasonable again. The incipient stage of the disease is important, I tell you. Should its first stage be neglected, the onset may be irreversible."

"It may already be irreversible," replied Takayanagi in a tone of desperation.

"That is your disease talking. Your disease is making you pessimistic."

"Pessimism comes quite naturally to a man without hope. You are not pessimistic because you have no reason to be."

"You are impossible," said Nakano, for the moment giving up on his friend. He stood up and opened the shoji door. The phoenix tree's leafless branches pointed to the sky.

"What a desolate garden! Nothing but a bare phoenix tree."

"The tree had leaves until only recently. How quickly things change. Have you ever seen the moon shining on a bare phoenix tree? It's a terrible sight."

"Surely. But you should not be sitting up on a cold night. I, for one, do not like the winter moon. The moon is best on a summer evening. Wouldn't it be delightful to hear a pleasure boat on a bright moonlit night of summer, and to have the boat rowed up the Sumida as far as Ayase, and there to float silver fans on the current?"

"What a fanciful diversion. Floating silver fans on the current, indeed!"

"You take silver-painted fans on the boat, unfold them, and toss them into the air one after another. They glitter in the moonlight and flutter down onto the water. What a pretty sight it must be!"

"Is that your invention?"

"It is said that men about town in the days of Edo would enjoy this elegant sport."

"Extravagant fellows, weren't they."

"I see you have a manuscript on your desk. Is that your translation of *How to Teach Geography*?"

"I have given up that translation. Since becoming ill, how can I do such a meaningless job?"

"Then what is it?"

"It is a work I started long ago but neglected till recently."

"Your novel! What is to become of your masterpiece? When you are going to finish it?"

"I want to write the rest all the more, now that I am sick. I used to think I would take it up again once I had more leisure. But I cannot afford to wait any longer. I cannot rest unless I finish the work before I die."

"To speak of death is very rash. I heartily approve of your resuming your literary work, but I must warn you not to be absorbed in it excessively; you will only exacerbate your condition."

"I do not mind exacerbating my illness so long as I can write, but I do mind not being able to write. Last night I dreamed that I succeeded in writing thirty pages of the story."

"I see how badly you want to write."

"Of course I do. Suppose that I cannot finish the work. I do not know for what I shall have lived. Suppose that completion of the work is beyond my power. Then I shall have been a good-for-nothing. If so, my life will not have been worth keeping by means of a change of air at your expense."

"Is that why you are reluctant to take my advice?"

"Well, yes."

"Now I understand. Is that your real motive?" Nakano asked, and considered for a while, then continued.

"Well, then, if you are reluctant to incur expenses for no useful purpose, I will have to think of a way of making those expenses purposeful."

"How will you do that?"

"Your present purpose is to execute your literary plan, am I right? In that case, I will bear the expenses for your change of air with the proviso that you complete your work during your stay somewhere for the benefit of your health. Zushi, Atami, anywhere you like—to recover your health free from all cares. But as your conscience will not allow you to simply recuperate at another's expense, you will resume writing from time to time, whenever you feel inclined to do so. You will come home when you have completed your work and when you have recovered your health. In exchange for shouldering your expenses, I shall have the pleasure of seeing your magnum opus introduced to the world. What do you say to my proposal? I will have satisfied my desire to assist you, and you will have realized your ambition. Killing two birds with one stone, wouldn't you say?"

Takayanagi pondered the matter for a while, looking down at his knees.

"According to your proposal, if I bring my completed manuscript to you, I shall have discharged my obligations to you, correct?"

"Correct. And at the same time you will have discharged part of your responsibility to the world."

"Then I will accept your money. There is the possibility that I shall die, having spent your money to no purpose. Be that as it may, I will try to write until my last moment, and if I write until my last moment, then surely I will be able to finish it."

"'Until your last moment' is too much! You will go to a warm place such as Sagami and write a page or two at your leisure. Remember, I attach no limit to my condition."

"Uhm. Without fail, I will bring back to you my completed work. I should feel ill at ease wasting your money without doing anything at all."

"You musn't think that way, I tell you."

"Fine. I understand. At any rate, I will go somewhere for a change of air. I will leave Tokyo tomorrow."

"You are rather in a hurry. But perhaps the sooner, the better. I do not mind your hasty departure, for I have the money with me now," said Nakano, taking out a threefold wallet of twilled silk and producing a bundle of bank notes.

"Here is one hundred yen. And I shall send you more later. But this sum will do for the time being."

"I shall not be needing so much."

"Take this for now, by all means. Actually this proposal originated with my wife. I wish you to take the entire sum in consideration of her good wishes for you."

"Then I will take the one hundred yen, but I shall need no more."

"Yes, please do. It is already wrapped in paper for you."

"Well then, please leave it with me."

"Then it is decided: you are to leave Tokyo tomorrow. But where to? Well, that is for you to decide. Please write to me once you have reached your destination. Since you are not so very ill as to require my assistance, I shall not go to the station to send you off. —Let's see. Was there anything else? I was in a bit of a hurry. The fact is I promised to visit a relative with my wife. She is waiting for my return, so I must bid you goodbye."

"Oh, leaving so soon? Well, please give my regards to Mrs. Nakano."

Nakano left with joy in his heart. Takayanagi stood and changed his clothes to go out.

He had heard of one hundred yen often enough, but this was the first time he actually saw it, not to speak of having the sum at his disposal. He had long wanted to write a work to do justice to his talent, and he had written a page or two in the scant leisure time snatched from the continual drudgery of earning a living. But as soon as he warmed to his writing, he would have to interrupt it, pursued by the threat of cold and hunger. At this rate he would be unable to do workmanlike writing in the foreseeable future. If he were to spend his days translating *How to Teach Geography* and do nothing else, he would be no better than a carriage horse driven about all its life, eating from its feedbag. He was conscious that within himself was an "I," and to die without giving expression to this "I" would be a great waste. Not only that, he would be ashamed before his elderly mother and the world. People treat him like a fool because, having no opportunity to bring out the "I" within, he would be a hack writer for a living, turning out a translation that any dullard could produce. Regrettably, immediately after he had heard Dōya's inspiring lecture, he had fallen ill. The doctor frankly said that it was the first stage of consumption. He had a presentiment that if the doctor were correct, there would be no help for him. While he still drew breath, he had tried sitting down at his desk to write, but he was racing against time, slow to build a defense when the wolf was at the door. Thinking of the possibility that he might leave nothing behind and disappear unnoticed, he became feverish. If he could only accomplish this single work, he would feel exculpated. To make exculpation, provisions were necessary. The one hundred yen provided today was worth a million yen in ordinary times.

With the money in his breast pocket, he walked around the room two or three times. His spirits were refreshed, his heart renewed. Suddenly snatching his hat, he flew outdoors to the busy marketplace of the last month of the year. Climbing the twilight Kagurazaka slope, he noticed it was not yet five o'clock. Some of the shops were already lit up by gas flames.

Over the entrance of Bishamon shrine, the huge paper lantern, now discolored, swayed gently in the gathering dusk, its year-end repapering neglected. At one of the booths near the gate, a sushi maker, one sleeve secured with a towel, vigorously kneaded rice in the palm of his hand. At an open booth, mackerel pike glinted coldly. Black socks were lined up along the road, the vendor standing by with his face half covered and his hands in his sleeves. How could he sell his socks like that? Takayanagi wondered. An old woman was selling Imagawa-yaki bean jam buns at three for one sen. Fountain pens at six sen, five rin apiece seemed too cheap.

The world is varied indeed. By tomorrow evening he would be a hundred miles away from here. The sushi maker and the old woman selling Imagawa-yaki would be nothing but a dream. After he had spent the one hundred yen, he would bring back to Tokyo something much more valuable than money. No one could know these thoughts. It takes all kinds of people to make this world.

Dōya-sensei will smile when told of his prospective change of air at the seashore. "Well, well, isn't that something," he will say. How surprised he will be to learn of tomorrow's departure. How ecstatic he will be to know his intention to bring home a magnum opus. —Fantasies bred more fantasies. Forgetting his illness, Takayanagi, with daydreams of the richest kind planted in his mind, arrived at the door of Sensei's home.

It seems someone had come to visit before him, but considering he had come all this way, he abandoned restraint and called out, "Hello!"

"Who is it?" asked a voice belonging to Sensei himself.

"It is I, Takayanagi. . . . "

"Oh, please come in," he said, but he made no sign to show himself.

Takayanagi entered the drawing room, and, as he had guessed, he found another visitor there. The latter was attired in an Ichiraku silk overcoat, a somber striped kimono and an obi of figured Hakata silk. He had a narrow forehead, high cheekbones and goggle-eyes. After greeting Sensei, Takayanagi silently bowed to goggle-eyes.

"How is it that you have come at this rather late hour. Have you some pressing business?"

"No, rather, I have come to say goodbye."

"Say goodbye? Have you accepted a post in the provinces or something of that sort?"

At the pause, the wife entered with tea. She exchanged bows with

Takayanagi and left.

"No, I am going away for a change of air."

"Then you are unwell, is that it?"

"I personally think nothing serious is the matter with me, but I am strongly advised to try a change of air."

"I see. Of course, that is the best thing to do, if your health is impaired. When do you leave? Tomorrow? Is that so? Then please stay, and we will have a long talk. But first I shall dispose of some business with this gentleman," Dōya-sensei said, turning toward goggle-eyes.

"Well, I regret having to say it, but would you agree to a postponement, considering the circumstances I have just mentioned?"

"I wish I could, but I have my own obligations as well."

"Then why don't you raise the rate of interest? Please take the interest and postpone repayment of the principal till next spring. Won't you?"

"You have been making interest payments regularly. If the money were lent for the sake of earning interest, it could be lent to you indefinitely. But . . ."

"Is it impossible to continue paying the interest?"

"I sympathize with your urgent request, and I would like to comply. But . . ."

"Is it impossible?"

"I'm sorry."

"Is it absolutely impossible?"

"I must ask you to come up with at least one hundred yen."

"On this very night?"

"Yes. Well, that's the size of it. The payment deadline was yesterday, as you recall."

"Yes, I know. I am not a man to forget the expiration of his debt. I tried everything to raise the money but failed in the attempt. I sent a messenger with a letter relating the honest facts."

"I thank you for your letter. According to its contents, you have a book manuscript you want to sell to a publisher. You want repayment of the loan put off till you succeed in the sale."

"That is so."

"But this money is not characteristically for the purpose of generating interest income. As a matter of fact, I expressly mentioned to your elder brother that the money absolutely had to be paid back by the year-end. He stated that 'Of all men, my younger brother will never break his word. I can assure you of his punctiliousness.' With his assurance, I accommodated your request. Your breach of contract will put me in an awkward position."

Dōya-sensei remained speechless, while goggle-eyes puffed leisurely at his pipe.

"Sensei?" Takayanagi suddenly interposed.

"Yes?" said Dōya-sensei, turning toward him. Dōya showed no sign of embarrassment. Had he a sense of shame about conducting business of this sort in the presence of a third party, he would have declined to see Takayanagi.

"Excuse me for interrupting your conversation, but may I ask a question?"

"Yes. What is it?"

"I understand that you have written a book. Will you kindly permit me to read it?"

"Yes, you may, if you like. Are you going to read it while waiting for this business to conclude?"

Takayanagi said nothing in reply. Dōya-sensei stood up, took the manuscript, about three inches thick, from among a stack of books in an alcove, and handed it to the young man.

"Here you are," said Dōya-sensei. On the cover page was the title, *Essay on Character*, written in block Chinese characters.

"Thank you," said the youth, accepting it with both hands. He looked closely at the three characters 人格論 for a while, and then lifted his gaze to goggle-eyes.

"Will you buy this manuscript for one hundred yen?"

"I am not a book publisher," said goggle-eyes laughing.

"Then you will not buy it?"

"You must be joking."

"Sensei?"

"Yes?"

"Please yield the manuscript to my care for one hundred yen."

"This manuscript?"

"My bid is too cheap, isn't it? I know it is worth ten thousand times more. But as your former student, I ask you to accept my offer."

Dazed, Dōya-sensei looked intently at the young man's face.

"Please let me have it. I have the money. I have the sum right here. I have exactly one hundred yen."

Takayanagi took out the bank notes wrapped in paper, just as he received them, and placed the package between the two of them.

"Accepting such a sum from you . . . it's not right." Dōya-sensei pushed back the package.

"It is quite right. Please just accept it. I was wrong. Please sell the manuscript to me. Sensei, I was once your pupil. When you were taunted by your students and run out of Takata in Echigo—I was one among them. Please, I implore you!"

Leaving Dōya-sensei behind in bewilderment, Takayanagi disappeared into the darkness of night. Instead of returning from his change of air with his own novel in tow, the novel that was to be an expression of his own self, this manuscript, a greater work, Dōya's *Essay on Character*, now pressed against his breast, would be a present to his friend Nakano and his wife in compensation for their kindness.

Translator's Afterword:
A *Nowaki* Causerie

Falstaff: What wind blew you hither, Pistol?
Pistol: Not the ill wind which blows no man to good.
—Shakespeare, *Henry IV*

*Aki huku wa / ikanaru iro no / kaze nare ba / mi ni shimu bakari /
aware naru ran*
What color is / that blowing autumn wind, /
that it can stain / my body / with its touch?
　　　　　　　　　　　　—Izumi Shikibu[1]

無題　明治43年10月5日
(Untitled *kanshi*, Chinese verse, composed October 5, 1910
by Natsume Sōseki in the hospital after severe stomach illness)

淋漓絳血腹中文　　　　　嘔照黄昏漾綺紋
入夜空疑身是骨　　　　　臥牀如石夢寒雲

I spat up streams of crimson blood, my bowel's own writing,
Rich patterns surging, lighting up the dusk.
By evening it seemed my whole body had turned to bone;
On the rock-like bed I lay dreaming of icy clouds.[2]

Natsume Sōseki was a man of letters. More than a novelist, he was a poet, painter, public speaker, and public intellectual. He established himself primarily as a novelist with the publication of his first long work, *I Am a Cat*, in 1905, and *Botchan* in 1906. These two novels brought him public acclaim and are still read and admired in Japan today, firmly esconced in the literary canon. In 1907, a turning point in Sōseki's literary career, the author resigned his teaching post at the prestigious Tokyo Imperial University and accepted an offer from a daily newspaper, *Asahi shinbun*, to serialize his work.

1. Jane Hirshfield with Mariko Aratani, trans., *The Ink Dark Moon: Love Poems by Ono no Komachi and Izumi Shikibu, Women of Ancient Japan* (New York: Vintage Classics, 1990), 134.
2. Burton Watson, "Sixteen Chinese Poems by Natsume Sōseki," translated by Burton Watson, in *Essays on Natsume Sōseki's Works*, compiled by Japanese National Commission for UNESCO (Tokyo: Japan Society for the Promotion of Science, 1972), 120.

With rare exception, all the literary production to follow would be published in *Asahi shinbun*: a novel a year (together with shorter works, essays, a travelog, and public lectures) until his death in 1916. The novella *Nowaki*[3] was published in 1907 in the literary magazine *Hototogisu* (in whose pages *I Am a Cat* and *Botchan* had also been serialized), and in June of that year his first *Asahi* novel, *Gubijinsō* (Wild Poppy), began serialization.

"Nihyaku tooka" (The 210th Day), a companion volume of sorts, and conventionally linked to *Nowaki*, which it preceded by three months (published in *Chūō kōron* magazine in October 1906), is nothing more than an extended dialogue between two men, Kei and Roku, as they climb (one wants to say "wander") the volcanic crater of Mt. Aso. *Nowaki*, twelve long chapters in length, is much more novelistic in that it has more characters, action, and incident, but it is the title itself that links it to "The 210th Day" because the word *nowaki* (野分 literally, field + to divide or separate) refers to the autumn wind that blows between the 210th day (counting from *risshun*, the first day of spring) and the 220th day, during which time farmers fields could be flattened and crops laid to waste. By today's calendar, the 210th falls around September 1st, and the 220th day, on or about September 11th, a period of violent winds and typhoons, and of potential crises.

The peripatetic characters of "The 210th Day" are a perennial occurrence in Sōseki's fiction, first introduced by the wise narrator of *I Am a Cat*: "The founder of Peripatetikoi (*shōyō-ha*) was Aristotle." *Nowaki*'s Takayanagi and Nakano also enjoy walking and talking, but their story, more involved than the plotless "210th Day," is about the interconnected lives of three men, all writers: tubercular Takayanagi, his former classmate, the dandy Nakano (they are recent university graduates), and Dōya, a former middle-school teacher.

Winds, storms, and other meteorological phenomena have long been used as literary devices to set the stage for, to presage, to parallel, and to intensify action of the novel and its characterology. A storm bearing a sense of crisis is also observed in the 28th chapter of *Genji monogatari*, called *Nowaki* and translated as "The Typhoon," in which not only are many buildings laid bare (thereby exposing Murasaki to the wandering eyes of Yūgiri) but also Genji's own heart and motives.

As Dōya states in his public lecture in *Nowaki*: "Today the wind blows hard, as it did yesterday. We are having unsettled weather these days. But it is nothing compared to the moral uncertainty you may have ahead of you!" The winds of uncertainty that bluster through the twelve chapters of Sōseki's *Nowaki* blow disease and death for Takayanagi: each time the

3. Japanese text used for this translation is Natsume Sōseki, *Nowaki*, in *Nihon kindai bungaku taikei*, vol. 25, ed. Matsumura Tatsuo and Saitō Keiko (Tokyo: Kadokawa Shoten, 1969).

winds blows he has a foreboding shiver, a consumptive cough, or bloody expectoration.

The only Sōseki novel except for *Gubijinsō* that has not yet been translated into English, *Nowaki* at first blush may seem a minor work (not only because of its length but also because it is not one of his newspaper serializations), yet it is altogether characteristically Sōsekian in style and content—in miniature, as it were. It follows the social criticism and consciousness established with *I Am a Cat*, *Botchan*, and "The 210th Day." This *parvum opus* is an important work because it encapsulates so many of Sōseki's foci as a novelist and as a public intellectual, which can be thematized variously in terms of his philosophical and literary concerns, his personal idiosyncrasies, and his writing as a window onto historical detail.

Always concerned with the subject of taste, and especially the artist as taster, Sōseki gave a public lecture on "The Philosophical Foundations of the Literary Arts" in April 1907 (only three months after *Nowaki*'s publication), the words of which resonate closely with Dōya's speech in *Nowaki* (and with William James, whom Sōseki had been reading):

> Now, those who apply intellect are people who elucidate the interrelationships of things; they are labeled philosophers and scientists. Those who apply emotion are people who taste the interrelationships of things; they are known as artists and men of letters. Those who apply will are people who improve the interrelationships of things; they are called warriors, statesmen, bean cake makers, carpenters, and so forth.[4]

Sōseki himself continued to make public lectures, up until two years before his death (as listed in the appended chronology). The Dōya-Sōseki similarities are striking. But just as striking are the seeds of other characters in *Nowaki* that are developed into full-fledged personae in later novels. *Nowaki*'s Nakano, the dandy, grows to full fruition in the character of Daisuke, the "arbiter elegantiarum" of *Sorekara* (albeit a much more angst-ridden and disturbed Nakano). *Nowaki*'s Takayanagi, aspiring writer and social misfit, develops into *Meian*'s Kobayashi, editor, firebrand, and provocateur. And *Nowaki*'s O-Masa, one of Sōseki's stock characters, the put-upon wife, sketched only lightly here, of whom is said "unless she succeeds in molding her husband's character to her liking, her life will not be worth living," becomes *Meian*'s O-Nobu, one of Sōseki's most vividly limned female characters, whose project is to make her husband love her absolutely.

---

4. Makoto Ueda, *Modern Japanese Writers and the Nature of Literature* (Stanford: Stanford University Press, 1976), 6.

The word *yoyuu*, leisure, occurs frequently in Sōseki's writing (Takayanagi complains that he could write his great novel if only he had *yoyuu*)—and is not just a frequent topic but also a school, *yoyuu-ha*, to which Sōseki's name is affixed (as is *shaseibun*, a realistic style and technique promoted by his colleague Masaoka Shiki), often used in contradistinction to the Naturalist School. Also associated with *yoyuu* is *kōtō yuumin*, a high-class idler, a dilettante like Nakano who has the wherewithal to pursue artistic interests at leisure.

As a window onto historical realities from the picayune to the pecuniary, *Nowaki* is representative of Sōseki's depiction of material culture, the cash nexus, the price of things. He vividly describes Japanese culture of Meiji 40 (1907, the novella's historical setting, contemporaneous with Sōseki's writing): Sōseki's product placement for Ten-mei-sui Eye Drops, the monopolization of free park benches in Hibiya Koen, the price of sundries ("Imagawa-yaki bean jam buns at three for one sen. Fountain pens for six sen five rin"), and of course the one hundred yen Takayanagi receives from Nakano (the plot device which brings the novella to its melodramatic close), which he in turn uses to purchase Dōya-sensei's manuscript, and thereby assures its publication and clears his sensei's burden of debt all in one stroke.

The popularity of certain aspects of Western culture in Meiji 40 is also presented realistically in the form of music (the concert at Hibiya park), cookery (the Seiyōken restaurant in Ueno), the "milk hall" (or "milk bar," as I call it), Nakano's impeccable Western attire (down to his leather gloves which he carries in hand), the smoking of Egyptian cigarettes, and more.

Personal idiosyncrasies and recurring themes in Sōseki include private investigators, mentioned in passing in *Nowaki*, for whom he perhaps neurotically seemed to harbor particularly strong feelings of distrust and dislike, who nose their way into many of Sōseki's novels (even making a Holmesian appearance wearing an Inverness in *Meian*). "Geisha and gentlemen," Sōseki's code word for class distinctions, are mentioned in Dōya's magazine article and appear frequently in Sōseki's fiction, culminating in a heated discussion on the subject between Tsuda and Kobayashi in *Meian*.

Takayanagi belongs to the category of "anguished youth," which was an abiding topic of import (together with morality and character) to Sōseki, who expressed an interest in writing something to, for, or about youth to his friend Takahama Kyoshi, who took over editorship of *Hototogisu* after Shiki's death: "These days, I'd like to write an article 'To Today's Youth,' or a novel based on this idea, and really focus on writing something about youth" (Letters, October 17, 1906). True to his intentions, Sōseki creates a scene at a milk bar in which Takayanagi reads "On Today's Anguished Youth" in *The World*, a magazine edited by Dōya, and also another article in the same magazine titled "Attachment and Emancipation." Through his mouthpiece

Dōya, Sōseki is able to make pronouncements that he himself will espouse later in his own public lectures such as "The Philosophical Foundations of the Literary Arts," "The Attitude of the Creative Writer," and "Imitation and Independence." Morality and character also belong to Sōseki's chief literary and intellectual concerns and are part and parcel of all his novels, but *Nowaki* stands apart as the most moralistic and perhaps the most heavy-handed. Sako Jun'ichirō went through the trouble of listing 153 citations of *jinkaku* (character) used throughout Sōseki's writing, 21 of them occurring in *Nowaki*, the largest number in any single work.[5] The melodramatic ending, in effect, hinges on character since it involves ownership of Dōya's "Essay on Character."

Names of thinkers, artists, and writers appear frequently in Sōseki's fiction. In *Nowaki* names such as Jean Gabriel Tarde (together with his concept of assimilation, illustrative of Sōseki's abiding interest in science and the social sciences[6]) appear alongside Holman Hunt and Prosper Mérimée, and these references, allusions, and intertexuality enrich his writing greatly. *Nowaki's* Nakano discourses briefly on the importance of the ring in Shakespeare, and readers of Sōseki will recall that the role of the ring is foregrounded in his final novel, *Meian*. Another recurring metaphor is *ana* (hole), which we see in the leaves of the phoenix tree in Takayanagi's garden that parallel his own deteriorating health: he says he is "riddled with holes." My reading of *Meian*, in fact, takes the topos of *ana* as its starting point to dilate on disease and desire.[7]

One particularly provocative and compelling reading of *Nowaki* can be found in Jim Reichert's analysis of representations of male-male sexuality in Meiji literature,[8] where he asserts that (to oversimplify a nuanced argument) Sōseki purchased wholesale the medicalization and pathologization of homosexuality that was the dominant discourse of Meiji ideology. In his view, Takayanagi is caught in a homoerotic triangle of desire, his affections torn between Nakano's friendship (who represents male-female love) and Dōya's "manly love of comrades." Takayanagi's tubercular, degenerative condition indicates that his affections likewise are a sickness. This might

5. Sako Junichirō, *Sōseki ronkyū* [Sōseki Studies] (Tokyo: Chōbunsha, 1990), 132.
6. "Sōseki was determined to theorize literature in part as a social phenomenon, one that must be studied from the perspective of the social sciences," says Michael K. Bourdaghs in Natsume Sōseki, *The Theory of Literature and Other Critical Writings,* ed. Michael K. Boudaghs, Atsuko Ueda, and Joseph A. Murphy (New York: Columbia University Press, 2009), 13.
7. See chapter two, "Reading the Diseased Body: Fissure, Blindness, and the Gaze in *Meian,*" in my *A Critical Study of the Novels of Natsume Sōseki (1867-1916)* (Lewiston, N.Y.: Edwin Mellen Press, 2005), 23–62.
8. Jim Reichert, *In the Company of Men: Representations of Male-Male Sexuality in Meiji Literature* (Stanford: Stanford University Press, 2006), 167-198.

explain why homosexuality is under erasure in Sōseki's fiction (although its homoerotic content is still debated to this day), and why sexuality in general is not only absent but also displaced by pathologies.

Love as a disease is most famously explored by Thomas Mann in his novels *Magic Mountain* and *Death in Venice*. *Nowaki* is in many ways Sōseki's *Death in Venice*, published five years before Mann's novella. Both works explore the interrelationships of love and disease and homoeroticism. Both works also explore the interrelationships of writing and desire and sexuality. Whereas *Death in Venice* is often considered Mann's most important short narrative, *Nowaki* is considered a minor work, as I have said, and is usually neglected in the critical literature. Both Dōya and Gustav von Aschenbach are writers, and the similarities don't end there. Greater similarities, however, exist between the consumptive Takayanagai and the ailing Aschenbach, over whom is lain the pestilence in the city and the decay of Venice. "That falling in love should be a disease like consumption" says Harold Bloom, "is a persuasive fantasy on Mann's part, and doubtless reflected his own barely repressed homoeroticism, the grand monument of which remains the novella *Death in Venice*.[9] Understanding that love is a disease is also essential to Sōseki's fiction.

Dōya-sensei's act of writing itself is eroticized and described in masturbatory terms: "In the act of writing he felt as if the fire of his enthusiasm would pass through his fingertips onto the paper so as to scorch it. If there is prose capable of converting a blank sheet of paper into an author's moral convictions, into sentences upsurging and drenched with sweat, that would be Dōya's writing." This statement is much more direct than T. S. Eliot's "O O O O that Shakespeherian [sic] Rag" in *The Waste Land*. And if writing can be eroticized, so too can the sensei-deshi (teacher-disciple, mentor-protégé) relationship itself. Even if one does not subscribe to Reichert's reading, one must recognize that the mentor-protégé relationship is a site for potential eroticism. "Eroticism, covert or declared, fantasized or enacted," as George Steiner points out, "is interwoven in teaching, in the phenomenology of mastery and discipleship."[10] Dōya seems obsessed with mentoring youth, and Takayanagi is obsessed with finding a sensei.

That erotic triangles of desire form the basic geometry of most Sōseki novels is often pointed out, and *Nowaki* is perhaps the first to explore this geometry, but not in the conventional sense of two men vying for the attention of the same woman. *Nowaki* contains all the marks of the later Sōseki: although the didacticism and melodramatic ending disappear after *Gubijinsō*, much of the recognizable language and style of the mature novelist is here.

9. Harold Bloom, *How to Read and Why* (New York: Scribner, 2000), 190.
10. George Steiner, *Lessons of the Masters* (Cambridge, Mass.: Harvard University Press, 2003), 26.

Natsume Sōseki's name, so far as I can discover, is almost unknown to English readers. Substitute Franz Kafka's name for Sōseki's and you have the opening sentence to Edwin Muir's 1930 Introduction to *The Castle*. Young readers may now know the name Sōseki from Murakami Haruki's *Kafka On the Shore*, whose eponymous fifteen-year-old protagonist reads the *Complete Works of Natsume Sōseki* while hiding out in a library. Perhaps this and other contemporary references, along with new translations such as this one, will encourage readers to find out more about Japan's most admired novelist, Natsume Sōseki.

Chronology

1867	Born February 9 in Edo (Tokyo), named Kinnosuke
1880	Enters Nishō Gakusha to study Chinese school of classics; later sells all his Chinese classics and decides to study English
1889	Presents "Death of My Brother" at Society of English; becomes acquainted with Masaoka Shiki; reviews Shiki's *Nanagusa-shū* (Seven Grasses Anthology), using pen name Sōseki for first time; writes "Bokusetsu-roku" (Record of Chips and Shavings)
1890–93	Attends Tokyo Imperial University, majors in English literature; translates *Hōjōki* into English
1892	Joins editorial staff of magazine *Tetsugaku zasshi* (Philosophy Magazine), translates Earnest Hart's "Hypnotism" (Saiminjutsu); writes "Rōshi no tetsugaku" (Philosophy of Laozi) and "Bundan ni okeru byōdōshugi no daihyōsha Uoruto Hoittoman no shi ni tsuite"(On the Poetry of Walt Whitman, a Representative among the Literati of Egalitarianism)
1895	Teaches at middle school in Matsuyama; moves into Gudabutsu-an ("Foolish Buddha" hermitage); lodges with Masaoka Shiki, together they convene haiku gatherings; leaves for a teaching post at Kumamoto 5th Higher School
1897	Publishes "On Tristram Shandy" in *Kōchō bungaku*
1900–1902	Sent to England by Ministry of Education to study English language and literature; "Rondon shōsoku" (Letters from London) published in *Hototogisu*; learns to ride a bicycle as diversion from neurosis
1903	Appointed lecturer at Tokyo Imperial University; "Jitensha nikki" (Bicycle Diary) published in *Hototogisu*; lectures on "Eibungaku keishikiron" (Formalism in English Literature) and "Bungakuron" (Literary Theory)
1905	*Wagahai wa neko de aru* (I Am a Cat) serialized in *Hototogisu*; "Rondon tō" (Tower of London) published in *Teikoku bungaku*, "Kaarairu hakubutsukan" (Carlyle Museum) published in *Gakutō*; "Gen'ei no tate" (Phantom Shield) published in *Hototogisu*;

"Koto no sorane" (The False Note of the Koto) published in *Shichinin*; "Ichiya" (One Night) and "Kairo-kō" (Song of Evanescence) published in *Chūō kōron*

1906 "Shumi no iden" (Heredity of Taste) published in *Teikoku bungaku*; *Botchan* published in *Hototogisu*; *Kusamakura* (Grass Pillow, translated as Three-Cornered World) published in *Shinshōsetsu*; "Nihyaku tooka" (The 210th Day) published in *Chūō kōron*; first Mokuyō-kai (Thursday salon) held at his home

1907 Short work "Kyō ni okeru yuube" (Evening in Kyoto) serialized in Osaka *Asahi shinbun*; *Nowaki* published in *Hototogisu*; resigns from Tokyo Imperial University and accepts *Asahi shinbun* offer to serialize his work; publishes first newspaper serial novel *Gubijinsō* (Wild Poppy); delivers lecture "Bungei no tetsugakuteki kisō" (The Philosophical Foundations of the Literary Arts), later published in *Asahi shinbun*; publishes *Bungakuron* (Literary Theory)

1908 *Kofū* (The Miner) begins serialization; delivers lecture "Sōsakka no taidō" (The Attitude of the Creative Writer), later published in *Hototogisu*; "Bunchō" (Paddy Bird) published in *Asahi shinbun*; "Yume juuya" (Ten Nights of Dream) serialized; *Sanshirō* serialized

1909 Essays and short stories "Eijutsu shōhin" (Spring Miscellanies) serialized, *Sorekara* (And Then) serialized, "Bungaku hyōron" (Literary Criticism) published; *Mankan tokoro dokoro* (Travels in Manchuria and Korea) serialized

1910 "Shuzenji taikan": suffers severe attack of gastric ulcers; *Mon* (The Gate) serialized; "Omoidasu koto nado" (Recollections) serialized

1911 "Hakase mondai": rejects government offer of Doctorate; delivers lectures "Kyōiki to bungei" (Education and Literary Arts), "Bungei to dōtoku" (The Literary Arts and Morality), "Dōraku to shokugyō" (Entertainment and Professions), "Gendai Nihon no kaika" (Enlightenment in Japan Today), "Nakami to keishiki" (Form and Content); collection of essays *Kirinukichō yori* (From the Scrapbooks) published; farewell to Professor Koeber, *Koeber Sensei* published

1912 *Higan sugi made* (Until after the Spring Equinox) serialized; *Kōjin* (The Wayfarer) serialized

1913	Collection of lectures, "Shakai to jibun" (Society and Self), published in *Jitsugyō no Nihon-sha*; delivers lecture "Mohō to dokuritsu" (Imitation and Independence)
1914	*Kokoro* (Heart/Mind) serialized; delivers lecture "Watakushi no kojinshugi" (My Individualism)
1915	*Garasu dō no naka* (Within Glass Doors) serialized; *Michikusa* (Grass on the Wayside) serialized; collection of essays "Irodōri" (Birds of Color) and "Kongōsō" (Diamantine Grass) published
1916	"Tentō-roku"(Record of Nodding) published; *Meian* (Light and Darkness) begins serialization (uncompleted at this death); composes seventy-five *kanshi*, Chinese verses, while writing *Meian*; dies December 9, buried in Zoshigaya Cemetery, Tokyo

Printed and bound by CPI Group (UK) Ltd, Croydon, CR0 4YY

09/06/2025

14685672-0002